"FATHER," ZIYAL INSISTED . . .

. . . her eyes very clear, "I helped Major Kira and the others escape from the holding cells."

No, no, this was one of Damar's silly accusations. This was a joke, and Ziyal was cheerful enough to help pull it on her father, her precious father who had learned to love her. Yes, that was it. She was joking, teasing.

Dukat swallowed, then again. "Do you know what you're saying?"

"Yes, I do," she told him firmly. "I belong here. Good-bye, Father . . . I love you . . ." She stepped away from him, putting a gap between them as if to declare her position.

No, no, this was not right. Dukat reached for her. He smiled, he took a step—

She gazed at him with the oddest expression. A crease of pain, wonder in her eyes, confusion . . . a flash . . . a gaping hole opened up in her chest . . . her arms flared slightly as she was propelled backward away from Dukat.

His fingers scratched the air to catch her, but she shot away from him.

"No!" he screamed.

STAR TREK
DEEP SPACE NINE®

THE
DOMINION WAR
BOOK FOUR

. . . SACRIFICE OF ANGELS

Diane Carey

POCKET BOOKS

New York   London   Toronto   Sydney   Tokyo   Singapore

This book is a work of fiction. Names, characters, places and incidents are products of the author's imagination or are used fictitiously. Any resemblance to actual events or locales or persons, living or dead, is entirely coincidental.

An *Original* Publication of POCKET BOOKS

POCKET BOOKS, a division of Simon & Schuster Inc. 1230 Avenue of the Americas, New York, NY 10020

This book is published by Pocket Books, a division of Simon & Schuster Inc., under exclusive license from Paramount Pictures.

ISBN: 0-671-02498-1

First Pocket Books printing December 1998

10 9 8 7 6 5 4 3 2 1

POCKET and colophon are registered trademarks of Simon & Schuster Inc.

Printed in the U.S.A.

...SACRIFICE OF ANGELS

CHAPTER
1

"BEN, COME IN. What've you got on the Argolis problem?"

The admiral's office was a mirror likeness of Sisko's, with the exception of personal items that implied a certain permanence. Sisko had deliberately not put any such things in his office, not wanting to give anybody the idea that maybe he liked it here and wanted to stay.

Despite his inclination to rush in early, he had waited until 0800 before coming to Ross with a battle plan he'd had ready for much longer, but that would've given too much away. And he had to be careful how he worded his plans to Ross.

Admiral Ross already had a star chart of Argolis Cluster raised on a wall monitor. After a polite greeting, Sisko went straight to the monitor—he didn't mind showing that he was proud of his work.

The star chart was loaded with the positions of the sensor array embedded into its program, which proved to Sisko that Martok had funneled the information through already and he could speak freely— more or less. There was even a set of faint blinking lights that indicated the fighter group of guard ships planted there by the Jem'Hadar. Destroying the array was one problem—those ships were another, much bigger, problem.

"All right, Ben, what's your plan?" the admiral asked. "How do we get an assault squadron in close enough to blast an array that can see them coming?"

Though Admiral Harold Ross was not a great tactician, he was in fact known for keen self-appraisal and surrounded himself with advisors smarter than he was, whom he drove relentlessly. He wasn't a very sharp or inspiring fellow, except that he never beat around the bush and was scrupulously forthright.

"We'll have to draw the guard ships away from the cluster, Admiral," Sisko began immediately. "My suggestion is to use General Martok and a small task force of ships, no more than five, to create a diversion big enough to draw off at least half of the picket ships. Then, while the Jem'Hadar think the activity's going on somewhere else, we send in a single ship to exact the assault."

"One ship to take down the whole sensor array? Are you kidding?"

"Not at all. The array can be neutralized with one powerful and cleverly arranged assault—"

"Gosh, I wonder which ship you have in mind, Ben."

Sisko turned to him and smiled. "You mean there's more than one ship around?"

"Okay, but you still haven't told me how you can sneak up on a thing like that, even with just one ship."

"I'll get to that right now, sir. According to Intelligence, the array is capable of detaching cloaked ships as far away as two thousand light-years. By the time the *Defiant* got around the Argolis Cluster, the Dominion would already know we were coming."

Ross nodded grimly. "You'd have more than a dozen Jem'Hadar ships on you before you even got close."

Sisko returned the nod. "We need to have the element of surprise on our side. It's the only way."

"What are you suggesting?"

"That I take the ship *through* the Argolis."

"You can't take a ship through there! You'd be cut to pieces."

"That's exactly what the Dominion thinks," Sisko told him proudly. "But if we came at them from the Argolis, they wouldn't know what hit them."

"What makes you think you can get through?" the admiral asked again.

"Dax says she can navigate around the gravimetric distortions. She's studied protostar clusters and she knows what to look for."

Ross glowered at the star chart, then at Sisko, then the chart again. He wanted to believe it could be done. Even more, he wanted that array shut down.

"It's a gamble," Sisko agreed to the silent protest. "But it's one I'm willing to take."

Troubled, Ross dealt with the fact that part of his job as flag admiral in a war was to take just this kind of risk, and also to trust the people he'd asked to give him ideas. If he didn't take suggestions, no matter how dangerous, eventually people would stop giving him their best ideas. They'd start assuming he wouldn't accept this or that, and they'd quit trying.

A recipe for disaster.

Stopping himself from pushing too hard, Sisko held his breath and waited. The admiral had the facts.

"All right," Ross said, "let's give it a shot. When can you leave?"

Sisko cut short an anxious step forward. "As soon as we've finished repairs on the *Defiant.*"

Ross shrugged with just his eyebrows. "Keep me posted."

"I will, sir."

With a crisp about-face that really wasn't necessary, Sisko bolted for the door and mastered himself only enough to keep from running down the corridor. In the turbolift, he tapped his combadge.

"Sisko to Dax."

"Dax here, Benjamin."

"How are those repairs coming?"

"O'Brien says we should be spaceworthy in twenty-four hours or less. We're also being re-armed and having our stabilizers—"

"Tell him to cut any corners he can. I want to be ready in twelve hours."

"Why?"

"Because we have a—never mind. I'll give you the details in person. We have about—"

"Ross to Sisko."

"One minute, Dax. Sisko here, Admiral."

"Come back to my office for a moment, would you? Something else has come up."

"Right away, sir. Sisko out. Dax, are you still there?"

"I'm standing by, Benjamin."

"I've just been ordered back to the admiral's office. Keep up the repair process and muster all hands for a crew meeting at ten hundred. Sisko out."

The turbolift almost got a hemorrhage when he made it reverse course all the way back through the interior of the station on express setting, but in less than three minutes he was back in the admiral's office—and he didn't like that. The longer he spent around Ross, the higher were his chances of blowing the delicate balance he'd set up.

The admiral had no secretary at the moment, so Sisko strode through the outer office and chimed the door, and was immediately admitted back into Ross's presence.

"You wanted to see me, Admiral?"

He avoided adding *again?*

Ross turned from his personal monitor. "I just got word. Captain Bennet's promotion came through. At my recommendation, Starfleet's putting her in charge of the Seventh Tactical Wing. She's one of the best adjutants I've ever had . . . strong grasp of strategy, and an ability to see the big picture."

Uh-oh . . .

Sisko knew he was sinking fast, but there was only one response for this—

"It doesn't sound like it's going to be easy to find someone to take her place."

Don't say it, please don't say it—

"I already have," Ross told him. "You."

Unable to keep his expression in check, Sisko tried to appear astonished. "Sir?"

Ross smiled—*Damn, he thinks he's doing me a kindness!*

"I've been very impressed with you these last few weeks. I think we're going to make a good team."

Sisko struggled not to groan. "Thank you, sir . . ."

"Your assignment is effective immediately."

Just before he managed a resigned nod, Sisko felt his spine go stiff with interior assessment of what Ross had just said. Starfleet lingo was like legal lingo—now meant now.

"Immediately, sir . . . what about the Argolis mission?"

"Commander Dax will captain the *Defiant*."

A cold pit opened in Sisko's stomach. A risky mission was one thing when he was in charge—but now, with the idea of sending his crew out without him, things clicked into place and the full measure of danger bloomed before him.

"She *is* up to it, isn't she?" Ross asked.

With an internal flinch, Sisko realized that Ross might be misinterpreting his hesitation as some kind of doubt in Dax's abilities. That's all they needed! To have a whole new command team assigned!

"Absolutely, sir," he pushed in quickly. "I'd just . . . gotten used to the idea of commanding the mission myself."

But Ross wasn't moved. How many assignments had he himself been forced to give up because he was needed somewhere else? Sisko knew that was the burden of an admiral, and a captain's attachment to his crew and ship just couldn't play too deeply into overreaching plans and needs. He also knew that Ross understood the value of that attachment and probably hadn't made this damned decision lightly.

He'd blown it. He'd done his job just a little too well. Impressed Ross with the plans for covert assaults, and now his plan for the Argolis mission had broken the fine structure he'd set up. The balance had cracked, and now he was going to fall into the fissure.

With a sympathetic glance, Ross motioned to several padds stacked on his desk. "Look over these tactical reports. I want your thoughts on the Bolian operation. We'll meet here at 0600 tomorrow morning."

With numb hands, Sisko picked up one of the padds and gazed at it.

Ross sat down at the desk behind which he himself was trapped. "Ben? Congratulations."

Forcing a plaintive grin, Sisko nodded. Then he turned and left. What else could he do? Argue?

Locked in at Starfleet Command.

What would he tell the crew? Go out and risk your lives in the most dangerous mission so far in this war . . . but go without me?

And what would he tell Martok?

How would he ever get back to DS9?

CHAPTER
2

WORF HURRIED PAST braised panels with equipment that sparked and snapped in his face and burned his hands as he passed. Several Klingons, injured or dead, lay crumpled on the deck. He ignored them all. On the deck five corridor, he found himself and a damage-control team stopped short at a locked conduit hatch. Ch'Targh and the damage-control team were clustered at the hatch panel, trying to get in.

"Report," Worf snapped to get their attention.

Ch'Targh turned. "We sealed the impulse injector, Commander."

"Where is my son?"

"Trapped in that corridor, sir. After we secured the injector, I sent him in there to put away the tools,

9

and somehow he tripped the emergency lockdown. We are trying to override it now."

An uncharitable round of laughter rumbled through the working Klingons. They had their backs to him, so Worf's scolding glare had no effect.

They were mocking him, yes, but not in private. In its way, that was progress. He had never taken chiding well. Other Klingons learned early to field such social irritations, but Worf had missed that. His foster parents had protected him from it.

A sudden stab of realization cut through his chest. The Rozhenkos would have also protected Alexander, without really meaning to debilitate him. Worf had been attuned to his own floundering, without considering that the boy might be floundering too, not quite as sure of himself and his actions as he tried so hard to appear.

Was that possible? Had the boy locked himself away by accident or by design? Was he merely a confused youth, strangled for attention? Trying any trick to get it?

Would he try such a trick if he had been tranferred to another ship? Where his father was not present as an audience?

No, Martok was right. Worf was the target of Alexander's actions. Clumsy actions, perhaps, but Worf knew he was as guilty of faltering, floundering, taking comfort in inaction.

Ch'Targh let out a victorious grunt, and the hatch slid open, spewing a gout of smoke, some cinders, and a small-boned Klingon teenager. Well, one-quarter Klingon.

Worf suddenly wanted to pay attention to the other three-quarters of his son.

Alexander faced him bravely and ignored the chuckles from the other Klingons, so effectively in fact that soon the chuckling died off and the others waited silently to see what Worf would do and whether Alexander would care.

"You locked yourself in?" Worf asked.

"Yes, sir."

With some kind of understanding, Worf nodded even though he didn't really understand, and put his hand on his son's shoulder. "Come."

Together they walked out of the company of others, whose opinions no longer mattered.

The others were silent this time. Something had changed.

"General. Thank you for coming."

"I come because two of my crew require my help. As far as friends are concerned, what a waste of time."

Martok chuckled out the last few words, and Alexander smiled with some embarrassment. Sitting opposite his son here in his own quarters, Worf seemed to relax a little too.

So, Martok sensed, the hard part was over. The two had reached some kind of understanding that they could not change each other and perhaps that wasn't the key after all. They had stopped trying and now would make headway.

"Please sit down, General," Worf invited. Since he didn't stand to greet his superior, Martok took that as a signal that Worf didn't want the advice of a superior after all, but an elder. Yes, a friend. But more—a *family* friend.

That was well. And about time.

Martok sat down and wished for war nog. Or something hot. Later.

"What can I do for you?" he asked, deliberately looking at Worf instead of the boy.

"My son is a man," Worf said. "I have been seeing him as a child. What other mistakes have I made?"

"You really want to know?"

"I would like your opinion."

"I would love to give it," Martok grunted. Now he looked at Alexander. "You want to hear also?"

The boy—the young man—nodded. "I'm considering becoming a member of your house. My father says it's my choice now. I'd like your opinion."

This was the moment Martok had hoped for. He had steered events and manipulated personalities in order to be asked to speak. Therefore he was ready.

"Then I will give you my thoughts by speaking some truths and by asking questions of you and requiring honest answers. Fair enough?"

"Fair," Alexander said. Strange that the surly youth had graduated to a young adult who wanted the air cleared. This was a good thing.

Worf only nodded once.

Martok hitched to the edge of his chair and positioned himself nearly between them, so neither would imagine he was on the other one's side. "Worf, you sent your son away many years ago."

"To live with my parents, yes."

"Humans."

"Yes . . ."

"Alexander, you lived with them and were content?"

The boy's eyes flickered, uneasy about this line of talk. "Yes, but . . ."

"But you wondered where your father was and why he failed to contact you."

"I wondered very much. I heard stories, but never from him."

"So you concluded because he was silent that he did not love you or care for you. Why did you think that?"

Alexander's expression turned harder. "Because he didn't send me away until I told him I didn't want to be a warrior." Now he looked at his father. "You were ashamed of me."

"I was never ashamed!"

"Worf—" Martok held out his hand for peace. "Alexander, did you prefer to be with your grandparents?"

"Yes, I preferred them! My father wouldn't speak to me once I decided not to be a warrior."

Martok let a moment of quiet come between

them, and let Alexander's revelation ring a little, and also waited for something more important—for Alexander to make contact with his father. And he did. Their eyes met. The shields dropped another ten percent.

Watching Worf, Martok digested the complete shock in his first officer's face and the corresponding realization there.

"Alexander," Martok said, "the word 'father' does not mean 'all-knowing.' Your father struggled long to be a warrior. It came more naturally to him, but it was still a struggle. He struggled so hard that there is little left in him that is not warrior. He is not always a Klingon warrior—sometimes he is a Starfleet warrior, and that is very different but he has the courage to be different. Still, he is all warrior. When you said you had no wish to be a warrior, I think your father had no idea what to say to you. When Worf does not know what to say . . ."

The boy looked at Worf. "He says nothing? Was that it? Because you didn't know what to say to me, you became silent?"

Worf stared at him, but in many ways was staring back at himself. "I had no idea how to cope with your choice . . . the choice, not you . . ."

"What your father is saying, in his lavalike manner, Alexander, is that he does not communicate well." Martok leaned back in his chair and forced himself to appear relaxed, signaling that progress was being made. In fact, it was. "When one is a child, everything your parents do seems intentional, doesn't it?"

Alexander twitched and blinked, hearing the unspoken answer.

"Even when they do something hurtful," Martok said, "or clumsy or stupid, you figure there must be a reason and this must be something they're doing on purpose. Not just because they fouled up!"

"Fouled up," the boy murmured.

"Of course!" Martok slapped his own knees. "You never thought about this. Perhaps your father is just terrible at being a father. Did you ever think of that? No, never. You thought he was being a terrible father on purpose! Because he enjoyed it! Parents can't be doing something that seems bad simply because they are incompetent, but on purpose!"

Alexander both slumped and gawked. "You mean . . . he . . ."

"I mean he is as clumsy as a fish when it comes to knowing how a father should behave. This has nothing to do with his love for you or his devotion or how he thinks of you, boy. When you told him you didn't want to be a warrior, he simply had no idea what to talk to you about. Not because of you, but because of himself!"

With the insight of a young adult instead of a boy, Alexander gazed at his father as if looking at artwork for the thousandth time and only now seeing the brushstrokes. Acrimony suddenly, visibly melted and sheeted to the deck.

"And you," Martok said, shielding his happiness as he turned to Worf, "are guilty of clumsy silence, as are many parents, but you also respond too much as a warrior. Life is not war, my friend, even when there is a war going on. Honor is not just fighting with your hands, but with your heart and your mind. Your son wants to be something other than a warrior, yet he is here. Why do you think he's here?"

Obviously struggling, Worf showed great promise by leaning forward and rubbing his hands as if to clean them. "If he has other interests . . . why would he come?"

"Why, Alexander?" Martok relayed.

The boy instantly said, "To do my part."

"Why now?"

"Because now . . . there's a war."

"Simple answer! Like millions before him," Martok said flatly, "he wants to do his part." He stood up suddenly and clapped his hands to his thighs. "Now you will speak as father and son, not as warrior and not-a-warrior."

Worf looked up in a panic. "You're leaving?"

"That's right. Sink or swim, my friends. I think you will swim."

When Martok left, Worf expected to feel empty, desperate, even frightened. But his son's gaze, like that of an equal, like that of an adult, gave him quick respite.

Somehow, the lifeline thrown by Martok was still

here even after the general's sudden exit. Worf at first hated Martok, then greatly respected him for leaving just at this moment.

He squirmed, then faced his son and settled down to speak as equals.

"I have been a poor father," he admitted. "You were right to be angry with me, but you must believe I always loved you. I always wanted security and attention for you. I sent you to my parents because they could give those to you. I never required you to be a warrior, Alexander—"

"But Martok's right, isn't he?" Alexander asked. "You don't know how to talk about anything else."

"I am not a very . . . demonstrative man."

"You're demonstrative enough to be getting married," the boy keenly noted, with a rumble in his throat that hinted at impending manhood.

Worf felt his face flush. "With women, things are different."

Alexander rolled his eyes and sighed. "I sure hope so. Father, I don't know if I will want to stay a warrior after this is all over, *if* we win . . . but I want to be a warrior now, so I can say to my own son that I did my part when it was important. Do you understand the difference?"

Gazing in fresh respect, Worf murmured, "You communicate very well. You speak freely . . . I should learn to respect that."

Alexander nodded. "I *am* demonstrative."

Sagging a little more, Worf pressed his elbows to

his knees and gazed at the deck. "I don't require you to be a perfect warrior, Alexander . . . but if you're going to be a warrior, you must be able to survive. For good or worse," he said, looking up now, "you joined the service and you must do a good job for yourself and your shipmates. I will help you. In return, I ask you to help me be a better father. Tell me when I am lacking, and I will work on it. There will be times when I respond as a warrior when I should be responding as a father. To you I grant the honor of . . . telling me."

Alexander actually smiled. "And to you I grant the honor of telling me when I'm a bad warrior."

"I have to," Worf told him. "I'm also your first officer."

"My first officer, my father, and a member of the same house," Alexander told him boldly. "General Martok thinks I've judged you unfairly. If I've been wrong about you, then I should correct the wrong. I have a wedding gift for you, Father . . . to show my respect and admit my mistake, I'll join the House of Martok."

Staring until his eyes burned, Worf absorbed the phenomenal depth of this gesture, this commitment, and quickly sifted the past few days to make sure he had not made any pressures or hints—no, this was all Alexander's idea, his own choice.

Worf lowered his head and shook it. "This will not be easy . . ."

"I don't care about easy," his son freely accepted. " 'Easy' isn't worth having."

Greatly cheered, Worf suddenly straightened. "That is a strong sentiment!"

"I can be strong when I have to be," his son said with a lilt that sustained them both.

"Yes . . . you can. Alexander, I cannot change the mistakes I have made, but I promise you from this day forward I will stand with you."

Unintimidated, Alexander said, "We'll see if you mean that."

As a bristle of resistance rose in his chest, Worf realized his son was probably joking, but that he also had a point. "Yes, we shall. What you are about to do entails a grave obligation. Do not accept it lightly."

"I understand. And I accept."

"Good. I will teach you what you need to be a warrior . . . and you will teach me what I need to be a father. Come."

A wooden case, covered with gold stencils in the ancient Klingon language, unchanged for nearly four thousand years.

Martok opened the box slowly, with ceremonial deliberation. The ready room lights were severely dimmed, making the candles on the table the primary source of illumination.

Reverently Martok removed the gray-and-black

crest of the House of Martok, first carved for the family of his grandfather, whose name he bore and had honored with his own service record. A rush of personal pride briefly overwhelmed the general, then he contained himself and concentrated upon the two men for whom the crest now made its forty-third appearance.

He held the crest above a shallow golden bowl which reflected the glow of the candles in its polished surface.

"Badge of Martok . . ." he began. "Badge of courage . . . badge of honor . . . badge of loyalty."

Ah, the old words. Shallow in their sound, they were deep in old meaning. He placed the emblem in the bowl.

Together with Worf, he chanted, "Badge of Martok."

Worf turned to his son. "Alexander, give him your dagger."

The boy flinched as if coming out of a trance, then handed Martok his weapon solemnly.

Martok waited through the hesitation, then took the dagger and sliced his own palm. Closing his fist, he squeezed blood onto the emblem. Forty-three . . . How full of pride he was! Even though he had no more children coming, his house was growing.

"One blood," he murmured, "one house."

He handed the blade to Worf, who cut himself in the same manner. "One blood . . . one house."

And now Alexander, who was not afraid. In fact,

he seemed eager to cut himself and shed his blood onto the shield. "One blood, one house!"

Satisfied, Martok picked up the jeweled decanter beside the ceremonial bowl and poured blood wine all over the insignia, until the blood from their three hands blended to a single shade. This was eminently enjoyable, this ceremony, this wallowing in tradition, despite his preaching to Worf that tradition was only a shading of their identity. Martok did like the ambience and the ties which this harkened from his memory. He thought of his father and his grandfather, and those were good thoughts for an old man to enjoy. He felt young again.

Taking one of the candles, he touched the flame to the liquid. The alcohol ignited instantly and flame rolled to the edges of the bowl, reflecting in the eyes of Alexander and Worf as Martok looked at them both.

For a moment Alexander seemed to have forgotten what to do, but when Martok turned to face him, he remembered.

"I will be faithful even beyond death!" the boy vowed.

The fire burned out—he had gotten the words out in time, luckily, or they would have to begin again.

"Now!" Martok barked.

Alexander's hand plunged into the bowl and he winced at the hot liquid, but pulled the insignia out and affixed it to his shoulder.

Beaming at the young man as if he were his own

son, Martok was pleased that Worf moved to stand beside Alexander as an equal, not before him as an elder.

The general drew a firm breath and felt young as he made the announcement that tomorrow all would know. The ship would know. The Empire would know. He would tell them all.

"Welcome to the House of Martok . . . Alexander, Son of Worf!"

CHAPTER
3

QUARK'S BAR. The upper level. An illusion of sanctum.

Kira Nerys leaned on the metal railing and looked down over the milling crowd on the first level. Behind her, Rom wiped a table, keeping true to his role as first brother and busboy to the irascible Quark, which allowed him to nurse his role as Federation spy.

He had the best qualification to pull it off—he seemed slow, dopey, and greedy, but wasn't any of those. Thus, the perfect disguise.

Any minute.

Below, several Bajorans were uneasily reacquainting themselves with the station, their mood subdued by the presence of so many Cardassians and Jem'Hadar soldiers. The Cardassians were having a good enough time at the bar and the dabo tables; the Jem'Hadar were inexplicably standing around watching, but never joining in. Kira saw Quark and several Ferengi waiters ducking about, serving customers.

Any minute now . . .

"There he is," Kira murmured. She stiffened slightly, then got control over it. "Damar's a creature of habit, all right."

Almost directly below her, Glinn Damar strode in the main bar entrance from the Promenade. He had a particularly annoyed expression on his excuse for a face today—good. That meant he was getting more and more frustrated with Dukat's methods of running the station.

Kira turned her face slightly, so that she could only move her eyes to pretend to be looking in another direction.

"After a hard day's work," she narrated, "he deserves his glass of kanar . . ."

Damar barked an unintelligible order to Quark, who moved behind the bar and got the oldest bottle of kanar. While taking a seat at the bar, Damar glared at the Jem'Hadar soldiers with unbridled contempt.

"Why are the Jem'Hadar always in here, he asks himself," Kira mumbled on, as Rom listened from behind her. "They don't eat, they don't drink, they don't gamble . . . all they do is take up space. Ah—

Damar asks his bartender if he found a padd he was working on the other day. He misplaced it, and he wants it back . . ."

"My brother tells the truth," Rom murmured back, watching Quark pour the drink for Damar. "He hasn't seen it."

Appreciative of the scowl Quark got for his honesty, Kira felt a little grin creep across her lips.

"Damar doesn't like that," she uttered quietly. "The padd contained a draft copy of a secret memorandum he was working on concerning the shortage of white. Without the drug, the Jem'Hadar will run amok, killing everyone and everything in their paths . . . If the Cardassians can't bring down the minefield and reopen the supply line from the Gamma Quadrant, they're planning to poison the last ration of white and eliminate the Jem'Hadar before it's too late. Rom . . . how *did* you get hold of Damar's padd, anyway?"

"I'm good with my hands. Here we go . . . they've seen him."

"And the Jem'Hadar Third motions for the others to follow him to the bar . . . they pause a few feet behind Damar . . . Damar turns, realizing there's going to be trouble. The Third barks again—and, lo—he's got the missing padd. And Damar, true to his nature, accuses them of stealing it."

"The Jem'Hadar didn't like that," Rom said, tense.

"Why's he pointing at the table?"

"Because that's where he found it. Right where *I* left it."

"Ah—the other Cardassians move to Damar's side . . . I knew this was going to work. The Cardassians and the Jem'Hadar may pretend to be allies, but they hate each other—Quark, don't get in between—oh!"

"Ow! . . . I didn't know my brother could fly . . ."

"There they go, Rom. Damar and that Jem'Hadar tearing into each other—I see a knife!"

"That Cardassian's pulling a disruptor rifle! He's firing!"

"One Jem'Hadar down!"

"The others are returning fire! Oooh—"

"This is bigger than I expected. They're rioting!"

"Me too, Major! Duck!"

Constable Odo and a handful of Bajoran deputies had apparently needed nearly twenty minutes to reestablish some sort of order in the bar, finally separating the Cardassians and the Jem'Hadar physically—which was no little trick.

Gul Dukat had listened in amazement at the report that there was trouble in the bar, yet somehow he wasn't really surprised.

Dukat stormed into the bar in time to see Weyoun dressing down the Jem'Hadar Third in the most aggravated tone the Vorta had used to date. Dukat had come to believe the Dominion's representative couldn't actually raise his voice, but evidently he could.

The brawlers were bloodied and bruised. Several Bajorans had been injured in the corona of hostility and were being tended by Bajoran medics and a nurse. Broken chairs, smashed tables—and scars of phaser fire. Weapons discharged. Unforgivable.

As he came in, Dukat almost tripped over an unconscious Jem'soldier who at second glance seemed to be dead. And over there was another. At first he was satisfied, almost amused, but then the crowd parted and Dukat saw two . . . three dead Cardassians.

Dead Cardassians! And no battle!

This fired a switch he had never felt click inside his head before. Allies . . . now they had killed each other. There was no treaty for this.

"Who started this! Damar! Give me a report!"

Still furious and yet somehow sheepish, Damar stepped to him and straightened to attention. "They stole my padd! There was critical information and they have no right under our agreement with the Jem'Hadar that they can look at classified Cardassian—"

"I don't care what they did!" Dukat exploded. "You shouldn't have let the situation get out of hand!"

Damar parted his lips and his mouth hung open, but there was nothing he could say to defend himself against a "you shouldn't have."

Just to avoid giving him the chance to think of anything, Dukat whirled just as Weyoun gave his final glare to the Jem'Hadar Third and said, "You're reduced six ranks."

Weyoun was upset—Dukat could see that. Of course he was. The Cardassian/Dominion alliance was jagged enough without incidental trouble. The Vorta turned to Dukat and very carefully controlled his tone as he came to stand near Dukat and made sure no one else could hear them speaking.

"How could Damar have been so stupid as to leave such an inflammatory document lying around for anyone to find?"

Dukat gritted his teeth. "Your men stole it from him."

"The Jem'Hadar are not thieves."

"And Damar is not a liar."

"Keep your voice down," Weyoun warned. "Our men need to see that we're still allies. Smile. Dukat—"

"I'm smiling."

"Gentlemen." Constable Odo stepped toward them, and suddenly Weyoun mellowed in a rather horrible way at the nearness of a Founder.

Dukat almost threw up.

"I suggest," Odo began, "that we get everyone out of here as soon as possible."

"Odo's right," Weyoun—of course—said. "Tell your men they're confined to quarters pending disciplinary hearings." When he saw Dukat bristle, he threw in, "We'll do the same. And . . . keep . . . smiling."

Smiling. How noxious. What sense did that make? Smile after an event like this. Mightn't it seem more reasonable to be displeased? What good was there in pretending?

The war had been going well enough, but not as well as Dukat had hoped. He was a haunted man, unable to gain release from the ever-present face in his mind. That face flickered in the beveling of his morning mirror. It blew by in the glossy black facings on the station's storefronts. A shadowy set of eyes and a firm chin showed in the orb of the baseball on his desk when he happened to turn just right. He was being watched, eternally watched.

And there was a voice, too. It came in every report about activity on the Federation and Klingon fronts. Significant wins were always dogged by hurtful losses. Scissorlike raids dotted the star charts and were impossible to predict or track . . . and in most of those, there was a report of a familiar ship making daring cuts into Cardassian and Dominion holdings.

Always that face . . . laughing at him. Murmuring predictions. Threats.

Why was Odo looking at the upper deck? There's nothing up there . . . oh, Rom, nervously finishing cleaning tables. That retarded Ferengi stump, why would Odo pay attention to him? Just checking the vicinity, most likely. Certainly there was nothing Rom had to offer. Was there someone else up there?

Irritated, Dukat dispensed with concerns about Odo and the upper deck, which couldn't possibly mean anything on a day when his own men and the Jem'Hadar had caused far more trouble than anyone else on a station of hostiles. That was not the corner from which he expected trouble to come.

In fact, the Bajorans had been annoyingly steady, as had everyone else on the station, give or take that little temper tantrum by Vedek Kassim which had ultimately come to nothing but her own crushed skull. A charming display of sacrifice, but ultimately fruitless. What the Vedek had hoped to accomplish was beyond Dukat's reasoning.

Well, the latest tally . . . one dead Vedek, two dead Jem'Hadar, three dead Cardassians. One embarrassed Weyoun.

Acceptable.

He turned and left the bar, followed by the phantom face in the curved rim of a table that had been sheared in half.

"Odo, you wanted to see me?"

Kira Nerys strolled into Odo's office, a little more pleased with herself now that she had talked herself into the idea that this was a real war and if the enemy died, well . . . then they died.

Odo was pacing behind his desk, and if his mask-like face had given her any hints over the years she had learned to recognize irritation when she saw it.

"Well?" he asked. "Don't you have anything to say to me?"

Tilting her head a little, Kira fished about with, "You mean what happened in Quark's?" When he nodded, she decided to take credit. "It worked better than I expected."

"I *knew* you were behind it!"

"Of course you did," she told him. "We discussed it at the last Resistance meeting."

"And I said it was a bad idea!"

"Yes, you did." Annoyed at the memory of his resisting the Resistance, Kira let her indignation show. "And then you walked out of the room as if there was nothing more to say. But Rom and Jake stayed and we discussed it. And y'know what? I decided it was a *good* idea!"

"So you went ahead and did it behind my back?"

"Why are you taking it so personally?"

"How do you expect me to take it? I spend my days sitting on the Council with Dukat and Weyoun, doing what I can to make sure Bajor survives this war intact. The last thing I need is to have you running around causing mayhem. Do you have any idea what would happen if Dukat found out you were behind it? It would give him all the excuse he needs to throw every Bajoran off this station."

"The Federation is losing this war!" Kira challenged, seeing in him the same complacency she had kicked aside in herself. "We can't just sit by and do nothing!"

Odo drew a long breath and tried to calm down. "There are limits to what we can do."

Kira could see he was trying to sympathize, and knew, unfortunately, that part of his motivation was keeping her safe—not all of Bajor or all Bajorans or the station, but just her. How could she be angry at someone whom she knew had those unrequited feelings?

"I'm beginning," she let herself say, "to think you shouldn't have agreed to sit on that council. It's as if you've gotten so invested in making sure the station runs smoothly, you've forgotten there's a war going on."

He appeared stung, and deeply insulted. "Are you questioning my loyalties, Major?"

Kira hesitated. She hadn't meant that, but as she spoke she knew that was indeed how those words sounded. "I need you, Odo," she said, rather than waste time stating the obvious. "The Resistance needs you."

"Answer me," he snapped. "Are you questioning my loyalties?"

"Of course not! That's not what this is about."

She drew a breath to say more, but the door opened suddenly and she and Odo both turned, surprised. There had been no chime, no request to enter. As she turned, a lump of worry settled into Kira's stomach—at least they had managed to keep up the basic courtesies on the station so far. Had something changed?

Outside the door, flanking the entrance to Odo's office, several Jem'Hadar soldiers formed two lines, but did not come inside. Had Dukat gotten fancy? Wanted an honor guard now? Or was this Weyoun, staging an entrance?

But the individual making an entrance scarcely needed fanfare—or guards, for that matter.

The masklike face and plain tan shift implied simplicity, but this individual, clearly a female, yet in no way a woman.

"Hello, Odo," the creature said. "It's good to see you again."

Kira's skin crawled at the sight, at the sound, of the female shapeshifter. These beings—all but Odo—gave her the creeps. They were just too strange, too illusionary. What she was seeing, she knew, was not at all the truth. A shapeshifter, a Founder. Weyoun's idea of a god. Kira's idea of trouble.

Had the minefield fallen? Why was this Founder on this side of the barrier? Was she trapped?

Odo . . . he was quite obviously rattled. In fact he was shaken to the bones. Except that he didn't have bones, but that was . . .

So much history here, such agony and joy, then more agony. This person could convince Odo, and once had, that a shapeshifter was somehow damaged by time spent among "solids." Were these the only two Founders on this side of the wormhole?

Kira almost spoke up, but the female shapeshifter barely acknowledged that there was anyone but Odo in the room. The female didn't look at Kira, but kept her eyes focused on Odo's, as if they were in a mutually supportive trance.

"Leave us," the female said. "I wish to speak to Odo."

Elbowing herself forward a step, and quite unimpressed, Kira sneered. "Do you?"

With her manner she communicated that she had no intention of abandoning Odo here with someone who could influence him so fundamentally.

For the first time, the female turned toward her, like a mannequin turning on a spit. The female gazed with those icy eyes, framed by the bony orbits of that expressionless, creaseless, featureless face. And in the eyes, there was expression.

"It's all right, Nerys," Odo said before anything came of the cool glare. "I may as well hear what she has to say."

Kira quite dismissively turned to him as if to make the female shapeshifter insignificant. "Are you sure?"

Hesitant yet somehow secure, Odo paused, then nodded.

A crawling awareness moved across Kira's shoulders. She was no longer an equal—she was the "solid" in the room.

What could she do? Odo could make his own choices.

But could he, her key ally, her friend, her secret admirer, her link to the Ruling Council . . . how much influence, how much remembering, how much sensation, how much intimacy . . . how much could he resist?

Pulled in two different directions, how much could one person take?

As Kira turned and stalked out of the quarters, leaving Odo to the mysterious influence of the non-woman, she knew that he was trapped as much as she, and she was trapped as much as the female shapeshifter. They were all trapped behind the lines.

"You called her 'Nerys.' "

Odo nodded at the female shapeshifter's loaded statement and reflected that the Founders were not so distant that they failed to note the difference between a first name and a family name in a culture so different from theirs.

"What of it?" he asked her. Admittedly her presence here both annoyed and somehow insulted him.

"You used to call her 'Major.' Using a solid's name denotes intimacy."

Oh—that was it. Odo had turned away from her, but now he turned again to look at the face so like his own, the plastic and formless humanoid echo, and suddenly understood why he avoided mirrors. "You're a long way from home. Here to keep an eye on the war effort?"

"I'm content to leave the details of the war to the Vorta," she told him.

"Then what brings you to *Deep Space Nine?*"

"You." She fixed her sunken eyes upon him. "I was trapped here in the Alpha Quadrant when Captain Sisko mined the entrance to the wormhole. I've spent too much time among solids. I came because I felt the need to be with one of my own."

Tender, but all lies. Odo returned her gaze with a cold glare. "That's ironic, considering what happened the last time we crossed paths."

"You caused the death of a fellow Changeling, Odo. Turning you into a solid was the only punishment severe enough for your crime—"

"And now that I'm a Changeling again, you come here as if nothing ever happened?"

"We've forgiven you."

A lump of resentment filled Odo's inner being. "Well, I haven't forgiven you."

She apparently thought she was losing control over the conversation, because she closed the distance Odo had managed to put between them. "It's time to put the past behind us?"

"What about the present?" Odo countered. "You're waging a war against my home."

"This isn't your home, Odo . . . you belong with your own kind, as part of the Great Link."

Her proximity was nerve-rending. He stepped back a pace. After the Founders passed judgment on him and cursed him to solid status for so long, he had learned who he really was—an individual. Now they held that alluring drug out to him again, now that they needed his influence here in this quadrant.

"I'm quite content here, thank you," he told her bluntly, and meant it.

"You say that," she insisted, "becaue you don't know what you're capable of becoming. Perhaps if we spend a little time together . . . you'll begin to understand."

Tempting, tempting—he gazed into the past, into the moments of fulfillment his form of life could have, a spreading, drunken euphoria with the merging of a million minds and the comfort that came from forgetting individuality.

Individuality was a responsibility, a moral charge. Who wouldn't take the chance to suspend such a burden? To forget there was tomorrow and Tuesday and Wednesday and things to be done? Challenges to overcome? Being in a group assuaged those burdens and suspended the pressures of being an individual. He had come to think of that suspension as lazy and lowering.

But as the female stood here, holding the drug before him . . .

" 'To become a thing is to know a thing' . . ."

His own voice startled him. Was she making him feel this way somehow?

" 'To assume its form,' " she continued, " 'is to begin to understand its existence.' "

Odo offered her a less malevolent gaze. "You tried to teach me that when I visited our homeworld."

"I remember."

"I didn't understand what you meant by it at first," he went on, caught up in reverie, "so when I came back to the station I got rid of the furniture I used to have in my quarters and replaced it with other objects. I've assumed every shape in the room . . . I suppose if it weren't for you, I would never have known the simple pleasure one can take in spending time existing as a stone or a branch . . ."

He flinched slightly, knowing how silly that would sound to any of his other friends.

Then he flinched again—he had just accepted her as some kind of friend. What was happening to him? Why were his limbs tingling?

She bowed her head slightly, accepting his words as gratitude. Perhaps they were.

"I'm glad you learned something from your visit." She moved closer in their minds, without actually taking a step. "Your arrival was a time of great joy for the link . . . and your departure a time of great sadness. If only you'd stayed with us, Odo—"

"I couldn't."

"You chose the solids."

"And I haven't regretted it."

"Not even a little?"

Why couldn't he lie to her? His chest was cold now too.

"I do think about the link from time to time . . ."

"It's there for you."

"I can't . . ."

"Why? Because of Kira? You still have feelings for her, don't you?" Through his silence, she seemed to deduce the rest. "She doesn't share them. I'm sorry."

Odo snapped a surprised glare toward her. He hadn't thought she knew how he felt about anything but the link. "Aren't you going to tell me that I shouldn't waste my time with a solid?"

"You love her."

"I wish I didn't." He gripped his hands and tried to feel humanoid, tried to sense the separation of his fingers and the pressure of imitation muscles. "I'm so vulnerable to her . . . all she has to do is smile and I'm happy beyond reason. A minor disagreement between us and I'm devastated. It's absurd! Sometimes I wish I could reach inside myself and tear out my feelings for her, but I can't."

The female managed a small smile. "Poor Odo."

"I don't want your pity," he quickly said, embarrassed at the adolescent nature of his feelings and his inability to mature them.

"I'm not offering pity," she said. "I have answers for your many questions. Why don't you ask me something? Ask me one of the many things you need to know for your inner sanctity. Ask me while I have a form and voice. Ask while we are separate."

That implied there would be another time, without separateness. Odo almost challenged her, almost denied her the prediction, but something stopped him.

Answers—to all the questions. Just a few answers.

He forced his voice up. "Have . . . have our people always been shapeshifters? Or was there a time when we were like the solids?"

"Eons ago we were like them," she said. "Limited to one form, but we evolved."

Her tone said not just "evolved," but "superior." He didn't like that.

"On the Homeworld," he pressed, "are you always in the link or do you sometimes take solid form?"

"We prefer the link. But occasionally it can be interesting to exist as something else. A tree perhaps or a cloud in the sky."

That didn't make sense. How could a shapeshifter become a cloud? Clouds were not a single object, but millions of single droplets. Could they do that? How would it be physically possible to divide to such a microscopic level? How could he ever pull himself into a unit again? Could such division occur and still be one being? Curiosity drove Odo to try imagining such a frightening change. A cloud—he thought that might be a shapeshifter's idea of death.

"So many questions, Odo," she murmured, amused.

"I'm sorry," he said. "There's so much that isn't clear to me."

Was there death for them? Should he ask?

"If you link with me," she offered, "everything will be made clear."

Promises pounded on Odo's mind at her offer. He had promised Kira that he wouldn't. How could he tell the shapeshifter that a verbal bond to a solid was holding him back?

"You have to understand," he attempted, "the link is very overwhelming for me. Right now, it's easier to talk."

"But words are so clumsy, so imprecise—"

"Even so."

"As you wish."

She paused then, waiting for him to continue his line of questioning, to search himself for things he wanted to know and ways to cram the bigness of his thoughts into the littleness of words, the widely inarticulate into the confines of linear sentences.

So he decided to start more simply this time. A place where solids had learned ages ago to begin any relationship.

"You've never told me your name."

She looked at him with a peculiar whimsy. "What use would I have for a name?"

"To differentiate yourself from others."

She managed a perfectly human shrug. "I don't."

"But . . . aren't you a separate being?"

"In a sense."

"When you return to the link, what'll happen to the entity I'm talking to right now?"

Her flat lips elongated into a soft grin. "The drop becomes the ocean."

A glimmer of that vague answer occurred to Odo, then almost instantly fled. For a moment he thought he understood, but like grasping at that cloud, he lost it.

"And if you choose to take a solid form again?"

"The ocean becomes the drop."

She apparently knew what that meant, but for Odo, clinging to the image was troubling.

"Yes," he murmured, trying to convince himself. "I think I'm beginning to understand."

Without pursuing the bizarre idea that he was talking to an ocean, he took a few moments to really try to understand the elusive concepts.

"Then can you answer your own question?" she wondered. "How many of us are there?"

With the force of a revelation, Odo said, "One and many. It depends on how you look at it."

"Very good. You *are* beginning to understand. But there's so much more you don't know."

"Tell me," he begged.

"Words would be insufficient. Link with me again . . . it's the only way I can give you the understanding that you seek."

"I can't . . ."

"Why not?"

"I promised Kira . . ."

"She's a solid. This has nothing to do with her. This is about you, Odo . . . what do *you* want?"

Exasperated, torn, his mind blurring to confusion and need, he intoned, "What I want is some *peace.*"

Her hand took his hand—he didn't stop her, didn't draw back or flinch away.

"What you need is clarity." Her voice was harp music against the quiet of deep space. "I can give you that . . ."

As the spreading euphoria clouded Odo's mind, the female closed her eyes and that was the last he saw of her before his own eyes drifted closed. There was not the usual darkness of decomposition, but this time a warm glowing silver light.

"Do you want me to stop?" she asked.

She knew the answer and he hated her for it. Hated her, loved her, wanted the melting glory she held out before him, that he so deeply craved and was so tired of resisting day after day, minute after minute.

And there were no more minutes, and no more days. They were energy, flowing like lava, peace, clarity. Rolling—

Nerys . . .

"What are you doing in here, Damar? Did Dukat demote you to security detail?"

This was Odo's office. So why wasn't Odo here? Like he was every other morning? Behind his desk, mulling over the situation and redistributing security around the station?

Instead, there was no Odo and Damar was here, talking to some Cardassian nondescript.

Damar turned to her. "What can I do for you, Major?"

"I'm looking for Odo."

"He's not here."

"Do you know where he is?"

"Yes."

Rrrrrrr.

"That's good," she popped back. "It's always good to know where your boss is."

Just the slightest inflection on the word "boss" and Damar bristled at the reminder of his position. Satisfied, Kira turned away to leave.

"He's in his quarters," Damar said. This time the inflection was his to wield. "With the other shapeshifter . . . jealous, Major?"

Annoyed that she had let him see her reaction to this, Kira fixed him with a glare. "Try to stay out of trouble, Damar. You don't want to end up on sanitation duty."

She left him before he could construct a winning quip and walked straight to Odo's quarters and chimed the door. Her arms and legs twitched with instinct. None of this was good. None of it.

No answer. She chimed again.

From inside, a muttered response. Good enough.

She walked in, knowing that Odo might as easily have said get away as come in. "Odo?"

He stood near the window, gazing out, as if not

registering her presence. He seemed serene, but somehow that was artificial. Was he drugged? Hypnotized?

Influenced—

"Nerys," he acknowledged, finally turning.

"I dropped by your office. Damar told me you were here. With her."

"She was here. But she's gone now."

"Are you all right? What did she want?"

"She didn't *want* anything . . ."

"Then what was she doing here?"

It was almost as if only one voice were actually speaking. Kira heard her own voice, but Odo's was like a whispering wind.

"I know how you feel about her, Major, but there's no reason to be concerned."

She stepped closer. "You don't know how much I wish I could believe that. You didn't link with her, did you?"

A frustrated breath came on the wind. "Actually . . . I did."

"You did? What were you thinking!"

A change came over Odo. He seemed to leave the dream behind long enough to be annoyed. "She didn't find out about the Resistance, if that's why you're worried."

"It's not," Kira lied. She dared not get into that one—just how could he possibly know the female shapeshifter hadn't sifted his mind while they were enmeshed in that liquid union they did?

Odo apparently didn't believe her. "The link isn't about exchanging information . . . it's about merging thought and form . . . idea and sensation."

"Sounds like a perfect way to manipulate someone."

"She's not manipulating me."

"Ever since the day you crossed paths, she's been lying to you," Kira pressed, "tricked you, sat in judgment of you—I don't trust her. And I don't understand how you can trust her."

"I linked with her. If she had some hidden motive, I would've sensed it. She's . . . just trying to teach me about myself . . . about what I'm capable of becoming."

"An intergalactic warlord, maybe?" Kira blasted before this turned into a therapy session. "Because that's what *she* is!"

Odo didn't even seem inclined to deny that or, at least, that Kira was justified to think that. "Who knows? By linking with her, I might be able to make her understand that the Federation doesn't pose a threat to her people."

Amazing! Could he really believe that the Dominion was waging a war against a power they thought might come and hurt them someday? Kira shuddered with frustration. How could she explain the nature of overbearance, tyranny, control, imperialism . . . he wasn't grasping those right now. He was lost in something else.

Kira lowered her voice, trying to find his plateau of common sense. "Do you really believe you can convince her to call off the war?"

Troubled, Odo paused. "If you could experience the link, you'd understand the effect it has on my people. You'd realize that anything is possible . . . I'm only beginning to understand it myself. Now that she's here, I finally have a chance to get some answers."

"Odo, this isn't the time for you to go off on some personal quest! There's too much at stake. After the war's over, do whatever you need to do. If you want to leave and join the Great Link, I won't try to stop you. But right now, I need you here. Focused." Encouraged by a glimmer of guilt, of responsibility, in Odo's eyes, she surged on. "Promise me you won't link with her again, Odo . . . not until this is over."

He turned away from her, thinking carefully, torn between his great need and his great commitment.

"All right," he said, very hesitantly. "I won't. Now if you'll excuse me, I have to get to work. I'll see you at the Resistance meeting."

He left her then, moving in a controlled but hurried manner. He wanted to get away from her. She knew the signals.

Kira didn't turn to watch him leave. He was in trouble and she knew it, and she also knew she couldn't do anything about it. What did she have to offer him that would stand up against physical and mental merging with the ultimate of wondrous fulfillment?

Nothing. He would have to find his own way.

"See you at the next meeting."

"Maybe," she murmured to the empty room. "But things are different now . . . and I'll have to be careful around you."

Up Guards and at them again!

The Duke of Wellington

CHAPTER
4

"ARE YOU TWO ever going to finish?"

"Just a few more minutes, Commander."

"That's 'Captain.' It's an old naval tradition. Whoever's in command of a ship, regardless of rank, is referred to as 'Captain.'"

"You mean if I had to take command, I'd be called 'Captain' too?"

"Cadet, by the time you took command, there wouldn't be anyone left to call you anything."

The banter between Dax, Nog, and O'Brien was usually a nerve-settler, but today as Ben Sisko stepped onto the bridge of the *Defiant,* he was reminded by the sound of the crew's voices that he would not be here anymore to hear them or enjoy them, to share their troubles or agonize in their losses or revel in their victories. He had been relieved of command, so that he could take more pressing responsibilities at Starfleet Command without distraction.

This was his last few minutes on the ship, and they were about to embark on the mission that had been his whole reason for wheedling an inside position at Command. This was *his* mission, and he would not be going. The mission was phenomenally dangerous, chance of success thin, and he wouldn't be there to share the razor-edged event.

Did they understand?

It would be unseemly, unofficerlike, to explain too much to them or to stand before them and wish them well while also trying to explain that he really wanted to go, that he didn't feel right that they were going without him, and that he was worried.

Negative thoughts wouldn't serve anything but his own guilts and fears, neither of which had any constructive bearing on what they were about to do. A former captain's duty was as important, at moments like this, as a captain's duty—to be sure the crew had ultimate confidence in the ship's unit as it existed, not as it had previously existed. To imply they needed him would have been an unconscionable breach.

"Come to take a last look around?" Dax sidled up next to him, offering that quirky grin which reminded him so much of his old friend Curzon Dax, back in the days when Jadzia . . . oh, never mind.

Too many lingering thoughts, too much reverie. It could only hurt.

"Not a *last* look, I hope," Sisko responded, then counted on her to understand that he was hoping they would survive the mission, not hoping he would be back—even though he was. "How are the repairs coming?"

Dax shot a glare at O'Brien and Nog. "Almost done."

O'Brien smirked and plunged back into his work.

"I wouldn't get too used to that command chair, old man," Sisko muttered. "When this war's over, I'm going to want my ship back."

"Fine," she said. "When this war's over, *I'm* going on a honeymoon."

"All done here, Captain," O'Brien called as he stood up from the auxiliary trunks.

"Very good," Sisko said, unfortunately at the same moment as Dax responded, "All right."

The moment was instantly gone, but all had heard. None would forget. The embarrassment was all Sisko's, though Dax, through her smile and shrug, tried to share it. He nodded to Dax and therewith gave her the tacit approval to give her own commands.

"Plot a course to the Argolis Cluster," she told her crew, "and prepare to depart."

Every bell in Sisko's head went off—get out of the command arena. Hand over the torch. Give her the ship she commanded. Give the crew their captain.

"Good luck," he simply said, trying to keep from giving a farewell speech that could just as easily be taken for a pre-eulogy.

He tried to go to the exit, but Dax followed him. "I wish you were coming with us, Benjamin." Generous, because they both knew that and she didn't have to say it outright.

Sisko broke his stride, but his throat was closing up. He choked out a quick, "You'll do fine," and continued into the turbolift, leaving Dax behind with her gaze drilling into his spine.

He tapped his combadge. "Sisko, zero bravo, K one."

There was no response.

He closed his eyes and listened to the hum of the turbolift, carrying him first off the *Defiant*, then back through the docking area and into the officer-only access.

When the lift doors opened, General Martok stood there, waiting for him.

"Zero bravo," Martok quipped. "I am summoned, and I am here."

Not particularly comforted, Sisko stepped out of the lift. "Unfortunately, so am I."

"Yes . . . I heard your ship is going without you. Most disturbing. What do you want me to do?"

"We're going to follow through on the tactical plan—distract those guard ships with as much trouble and mayhem as you can. Get as many of them as possible to abandon the Argolis sensor array."

"I will," the general said. "But they will not all come away."

"I know that. That's why I'm taking another ship and going in there to help you pull them off."

Martok sat back and blinked. "The admiral's new adjutant is leaving his desk? With or against orders?"

"Well . . . a little of both. The admiral already took me off command of *Defiant* and he can't undo that arbitrarily, but I can get leaves of absence at key points, and this is a key point."

"How did you convince Admiral Ross of such an arrangement?"

"Oh, somehow he got the idea that somebody would be ringing his emergency alarm every hour on the hour until he let me go."

"I . . . would never blame him for such circumspection."

"So I'm going."

"On what ship?"

"Centaur."

"Captain Reynolds."

"Yes."

"And does the captain understand the level of our involvement?"

"Not a bit. What I need from you is the identification numbers off those guard ships at the array. We have to be absolutely certain that any ships we draw to the area of distraction are in fact the very ships that would be shooting at *Defiant* if we weren't causing trouble nearby. As long as Dax has the element of surprise, she'll handle the sensor array."

Sisko drew a deep breath after all those hopeful sentences and steadied his cold nerves. Somehow all this seemed too simple, too easy, and none of it would be either of those. The bedamned complication of being Ross's full adjutant required him to juggle too many glass balls. Despite his attraction to Dax's mission, other things couldn't be ignored. The last few days had been a scramble to reassign or retire problems and duties so he could be ready to go out with Charlie Reynolds on the *Centaur* and do what he had to do.

Martok had been silent for the past few seconds, but Sisko constantly felt the canny gaze of the Klingon general, who missed very little on the subtle plane. Unlike most Klingons, Martok was aware of underlying worries, motives, desires, and he had patience to see how those faculties evolved.

So he was looking at Sisko, and waiting. Sisko knew the questions Martok wanted to ask, would have to ask in order to pursue the mission effectively.

"You'll need a target for your distraction maneuver," Sisko offered without having to be asked. "We destroyed the main ketracel-white facility the Dominion had on this side of the wormhole, and that crippled them badly. They're staying crippled as long as the wormhole stays mined. That makes any repository of ketracel white very valuable to them."

"You have found another facility?" Martok asked.

"Not a manufacturing plant, but a storage barge. It's close enough to the Argolis Cluster that the ships guarding the sensor array might be drawn off if we stage an attack on the barge."

Suddenly eager, Martok leaned forward and glared at him. "This is remarkable news! How have they hidden this barge?"

"It's not a Dominion or Jem'Hadar barge. It's an old Federation barge they confiscated." A little embarrassed, Sisko shrugged. "We just didn't bother checking out our own ship configuration. They've never done that before."

Agreeing with a nod, Martok remained silent.

"I can't give you any more information," Sisko went on, "until we're closer to the source. The barge is heavily guarded by planetary salvos from the planet it's orbiting."

"Can we destroy the barge?"

"We can certainly try, but I doubt we'll succeed. That's not going to be my goal. I want the ID numbers off any ships that come in. Then we'll have to line them up and fight until we attract at least half of the guard ships from the array."

"Very well, my friend. This is a strange day."

"Yes, it is." Unwilling to talk about this anymore until the mission was under way, Sisko shifted gears and asked, "How are things on *Rotarran,* General? I understand you got a whole rank of new recruits."

"Fine young Klingons," Martok said. "Including one you may know. Alexander Roshenko."

Sisko snapped him a look. "Worf's son? He signed up?"

"He did. There were jagged moments, but we may have a warrior someday. He has shed too little blood in his life."

Those simple sentences, Sisko knew, implied much more stress than Martok would ever say. There was some poetry in the phrase "too little blood," commenting about the fact that Alexander had been protected through much of his life from the harshness of life as a Klingon in Klingon society. He was a part human, part Klingon boy who now, apparently, wanted to live in the Klingon sphere, but like his father had been raised somewhere else and now had a great struggle ahead.

Worf had embraced Klingon ways too much, then had to pull back and find the place in his mind and soul where he was no particular cultural possession, but an individual. He was still fighting with that, Sisko knew, and also knew that Dax enjoyed teasing him about it with regard to their impending marriage ceremony. Worf wanted all the trappings of Klingon tradition, as if he were desperate to show his willingness to do the surface things if only he could reserve individuality for the times that really counted.

Sisko inwardly flinched. He was involving himself

again in the lives of the crew who were no longer his to command. Worf was on Martok's ship now. O'Brien and Nog and Bashir and the others—they were on Dax's ship now. If they died on this mission, he wouldn't know it until long after.

If they even turned up missing in space, he'd have to send somebody else on the search mission. He couldn't justify abandoning his responsibilities as Ross's adjutant to run the search himself—and the reason would be that the *Defiant* had gone out on a high-risk mission in hostile space and was probably destroyed. They weren't just going on a picnic and getting lost in the woods. He would be forced by convention to assign the search to a border cutter. He couldn't justify going himself. Some strings were just too taut to pull.

"If we're not killed at the barge," Sisko said, turning to his friend and comrade in silence, "I'll have to come back here immediately. I won't be able to stay out there and keep an eye on the *Defiant*. We're going to lose contact with them when they ram through the cluster. I won't be able to stay and search for them. I'm asking you to monitor all the signals as long as you can, General. Do everything you can for them. They're more than just my friends and my crew. They're the alliance's best hope. So far we've been holding on, but we can't win a war that way. Holding on costs too much and we're slipping. We've got to start making real progress. We've got to start hurting the enemy. We've got to start reclaiming what's ours. We've got to go out there, General. We've got to find that barge and fight a losing battle as long as it takes. We've got to distract as we have never distracted before."

Glancing up from the crate of new glassware he was unpacking, Quark surveyed his realm. A quiet day at the bar. The place wasn't completely put back together, but at least all the new tables were finally being delivered and most of the blood had been scrubbed off the floor. Most of it.

A few patrons muddled about among the waiters who were rearranging the tables. So far, so good, except that he was beginning to prefer the place empty than crowded with the people who had been around here lately. Now, there was a dumb thought. Prefer the place empty. He was slipping, no doubt about it.

Uch—here came Damar.

What did he want? Why was he in here so much lately? Start another fight?

"Pardon our appearance," Quark said with unshielded sarcasm. "We're renovating."

Damar slung his leg over a barstool. "Kanar—not that one. The twenty-seven."

"The twenty-seven?" Quark waited for a confirming nod, then fished to the back of the shelf for the gilded decanter with the fluted neck. "Expensive."

"I can afford it," Damar said, "on a gul's salary."

Quark halted in the middle of dusting the decanter. "Wait a minute! You start a fight in my bar and you're getting promoted? What kind of way is that to run an army!"

"Dukat isn't happy about what happened. I had to find some way to make it up to him."

"Mmm—let's hope it was something big."

With a prideful smirk, Damar hedged, "Let's just say, it's going to change the course of history."

Quark uncorked the decanter, but was actually involved in Damar's expression and the glitter of self-satisfaction he saw there. The Cardassian was obviously up to something that could only be bad for the Federation.

So? What difference did it make?

The internal question very abruptly answered itself.

Giving the decanter a swish, he pressed up to the bar to pour Damar's glass of expensive twenty-seven. "As a businessman, I'm very interested in the course of history . . . this one's on me."

Damar smiled, leering at Quark in a way that suggested he knew Quark was trying to snitch information. "That's very kind of you, Quark," he said, "but I can't talk about it."

Quark shrugged. "Of course. I understand. Enjoy your drink."

Leaving well enough alone, he topped off the drink after Damar's first sip, then turned to rearrange the bottles on the bar.

"Let me share that with you." Quark poured himself a glass from the decanter. "It's not every day somebody comes in here who can appreciate a bottle of twenty-seven kanar."

"I thought bartenders didn't drink," the Cardassian claimed.

"Oh, that's just a legend. Us bartenders, we're the ones who really know how to discriminate. We're experts in our field. How else could we become experts if we didn't sample our wares? Does the scientist never experiment? Does the clergy never pray? Here, let me fill yours up again. Ah . . . mine too . . ."

The potent brew instantly sent fumes racing through his sinuses, directly into his cranial structure. Good, good stuff. It worked a little faster on Ferengi than Cardassian, but soon it would soak into Damar's thick hide and he'd start to feel the effects.

He smiled and nodded companionably at Damar, who was savoring the kanar. Damar's kanar. That was funny. Damar's twenty-seven kanars. Pretty soon, with a little luck, Quark would see twenty-seven Damars drinking twenty-seven kanars. That was funny too.

Another drink to wash down that picture.

Oh, too late. The Damars were replicating. Another drink to blur his eyes.

"I'm leaving now," he said to the three Damars

who were already sitting there. "You fellas enjoy your kanars. You just keep on drinking. And just tell me later what you owe me."

"You trust me for that?" Damar asked.

"Of course I trust you! We're at war, we're not uncivilized! You're a Cardassian officer! I mean, I wouldn't want my daughter to . . . but trust? Sure! You Damars keep enjoying your kanars and I'll be back in a while. Damars and kanars . . . y'know, it really is funny."

"You know what, Quark?" Damar rolled his unfocused eyes. "I think . . . I trust you too."

"Well, that's no surprise," Quark snipped. "It's amazing what a little encouragement can do. I'm a very trustable guy."

"You are . . ." Damar gazed at him in pure wonderment. "I never noticed before . . . you're like a doctor or a . . . a father."

"That's right. I'm your father. You can tell me anything. Anything at all. In fact, you know what? You *have* to tell me your innermost secrets. You *must* tell me . . . or trust is nothing between us and I'll have to just . . . never speak to you again."

"No!" Almost coming off his stool, Damar grasped Quark's arm. "No . . . stay, please stay. Stay and I'll tell you how history will change."

"Okay." Pour two more glasses full, blink, clear the throat, tilt the best ear forward. "Have a little more. That's right. Savor it . . . swallow it . . . good

62

boy. Now . . . tell me . . . how are you going to get that promotion we both know you so richly deserve?"

Damar glanced around, pretending he could see through his blue-rimmed drunken eyes, clutched his glass, and turned to the new savior of his universe, the holy high Quark.

"I . . . have figured out a way . . . to bring down the moan feld."

Quark stood back. "The moan feld?"

"That's right. The mean fold."

"Mean fold . . . oh . . . are you sure?"

"Absolutely. I had to do something, so this is what I did. I went around and gathered up all the deflector energy ratios on those moans, and I . . . thought of something. It can work. Dukat's ordered the engineers to start field tests."

Quark shook his head and filled Damar's glass. "Defecting. That's a serious business. I mean, running out on people who've been counting on you . . ."

"That's right, and we can use the station's array to do it, too."

"Now, *this* impresses me. I always had faith in you. Now, and only now, I understand why Gul Dukat relies on you so much, Damar. If you weren't a malleable sot right now, why, I'd get down on six of my knees and worship the slime you crawled out of. But, listen, I gotta go."

Disappointment creased Damar's scales. "So soon?"

"Oh, I'll be back. And this decanter of twenty-seven . . . I'm going to put it right over there, on a special shelf. Nobody but me ever touches that shelf. That'll be the Damar bottle. The Damar kanar. After you're finished with your drink, you go have a nice nap and forget you ever talked to me."

"That's what I'm going to do."

"Oh, I know you will. Have a nice afternoon, Damar, you dirty gray snake."

"You too, Cork."

Ah, the Promenade. What a wonderful place. The walk around the ring cleared Quark's head a little, but by the time he found Kira's quarters—when had this door been moved?—he felt as if somebody were behind him, pushing. *Ding ding.*

"Come in."

Quark melted through the door, thinking he was very upright indeed for a person with a slug of the good stuff smarming around his sinuses.

Oh, good. The whole team. Kira, Odo, Jake, and Rom. What an adorable ugly bunch of life-forms.

"Brother!" Rom looked surprised. "Are you all right?"

"No," Quark admitted. "I'm not all right. I just shared a bottle of kanar with Damar. That rhymes."

"You're drunk." Who was that? Three Jake Siskos.

"Of course I'm drunk," Quark told them. "I

wouldn't risk coming here and associating myself with your little 'Resistance cell' if I wasn't drunk!"

The two Kiras over there gave him a scolding glare. "Maybe you should leave before someone sees you."

Right. Leave. Good. He sat down.

"I've tried," he sighed, and shook his swimming head. "I've tried my best to run my establishment under this occupation. But y'know what? It's no fun!"

They stared at him, the whole roomful of them, and he lowered his voice so none of the Cardassians flapping around the ceiling would be able to hear. "I don't like Cardassians . . . they're mean and they're arrogant . . . and I can't *stand* the Jem'Hadar! They're creepy! They just stand there like statues, staring at you." The memory brought a shiver, and he blinked. "I've had it. I don't want to spend the rest of my life doing business with these people. I want the Federation back." Raising his hands to the gods of barkeeping, he wailed, "I want to sell root beer again!"

"All right," one of the Kiras said. "You've made your point."

"How can I relax when thousands of Jem'Hadar ships are sitting on the other side of the wormhole, waiting to come through?"

"Don't worry about it," Jake number two said. "They're stuck there."

"Not if what Damar told me is true."

Ah, they were amazed! They wondered how he got Damar to talk to him, to trust him. He couldn't tell them, of course, about the vial of red powder, but that didn't matter anyway.

"What are you talking about?" Kira demanded.

Quark turned to her. Where was she, anyway? Oh, right there.

"He said he came up with a way to deactivate the mines. Dukat wants him to start field tests right away."

They thought he was brilliant. He could tell because the whole crowd was just gawking at him with their eyes big and their mouths open and they were too stunned to applaud.

"Well?" he prodded. "Are you just going to sit there? Or are you going to do something about it?"

The crowd went wild. Cheering and whooping and patting him on the back. Then somebody shoved a hot mug into his hand. What was this stuff?

Coffee?

"Drink it!"

"Okay, don't push . . ."

"Come on, Quark, think!" Kira hovered a couple of inches from his face. "It's important! Did Damar say anything about *how* he was planning to deactivate the mines?"

"Yes. He said something about the station's defector."

66

Kira looked at Odo, who leaned forward and repeated, "A defector?"

"That's impossible," Kira said. "The only person on the station who knows anything about how the mines work is . . ."

"Me," Rom confirmed. Then he paused, as everybody suddenly looked at him.

But something was moving around inside the fumes in Quark's head and he held up a hand. "Defector . . . that doesn't sound right. Maybe he said *deflector*. Yeah, that's it! He's going to use the station's *deflector* array."

Kira turned. "What do you think, Rom?"

Quark's brother looked troubled. "I'm glad it wasn't me—"

"About the deflector array! Is there any way to use it to deactivate the mines!"

"No." Rom sounded confident. "I designed the mines to be self-replicating. The only way to keep them from replacing themselves is to isolate them in an antigraviton beam. The deflector array can't do that."

Good. Problem solved. Quark took another suck on the coffee—disgusting stuff, but something about it made him keep drinking. Kind of like the kanar with the red stuff in it—

"Unless . . ."

He looked up. Had Rom said something else?

Rom was staring at the chair Quark was sitting in.

"Unless you reconfigured the field generators . . . and refocused the emitters . . . which would turn the deflector array into one big antigraviton beam . . ."

Quark reacted to a surge of clear-headed frustration. "Why didn't you think of that when you set up the mine field!"

"I don't know . . ."

"He doesn't *know!*"

"Quark." Kira cut him off, still looking at Rom. "How can we disable the deflector array?"

With a flicker of hope, Rom said, "All you have to do is access the EPS feed and overload the waveguide."

"Let's do it!"

"But there's no way to *get* to the EPS feed. It's in a secured conduit rigged with alarms."

"Odo." Kira turned quickly. "Can you disable those alarms?"

"I can take them off-line for about five minutes if I run a security diagnostic."

"Rom, will that give you enough time?"

"I think so—"

"All right, you and I will meet here. Odo, at exactly 0800, you'll begin the diagnostic. Any questions?"

Sensitive to the urgency in her voice, Quark put down his coffee cup. "Yes. When will Rom be back at work? I have ten crates of *yamok* sauce that need to be unpacked. I have to keep that bar open, you know! It's critical to the future of the alliance! Well? What are you looking at me like that for?"

"Odo should be on his way to his office by now. Remember, he's going to interrupt the sensor alarms at exactly eight hundred hours."

"I'll be ready."

"I'll contact you if there's a problem."

Kira pulled the hatch cover off the access conduit in the second habitat ring corridor. This was as close as she and Rom could get to the deflector array controls without anyone's becoming suspicious or going into an obviously restricted area. Bad enough they were carrying a basket of fruit to disguise Rom's tools, but that was apparently the best Rom could think of. An engineer, yes. A master of deception . . . not really.

Rom climbed into the conduit, taking the fruit basket with him.

"Good luck with your delivery," Kira told him, and shoved the hatch cover back into place.

She tapped her combadge. "Computer, give me the time."

"Seven hundred hours, fifty-eight minutes."

That gave Rom two minutes to get to the deflectors. Hurrying back down the corridor, Kira made her way quickly—but not too quickly—toward the security office. She tried to keep any emotion out of her face that might imply she was happy—yes, she was. Happy that her little Resistance could do something to slow down the Dominion's takeover of this quadrant. Happy that Odo seemed to be still with them, despite his involvement with the female shapeshifter, whom Kira trusted no farther than she could spit.

Seven hundred fifty-nine . . . so far, so good.

Without bothering to chime the security office door and interrupt Odo from doing what they had agreed he would do, she strode straight in and parted her lips to tell him that everything was going as planned.

Except there was no one to tell. The room was quiet, as usual, but held a lonely chill. Odo wasn't here.

"Odo?" Quickly she slapped her combadge. "Kira to Odo."

She waited—only a few seconds to go. Rom would be getting close to . . .

The combadge was silent.

"Kira to Odo! Please respond!"

Silence. Deadly silence.

"Odo!"

Cannon to the left of them,
Cannon to the right of them,
Cannon in front of them,
  Volley'd and thunder'd . . .

CHAPTER 5

"COMPUTER, TIME!"

"Seven hundred hours, fifty-nine minutes."

"Kira to Rom—"

"Hello, Major."

She swung around, cutting off her own call to Rom, and it was a good thing, for here was Damar, glaring down at her.

"Just the person I was looking for," he said.

Now what? Less than thirty seconds to go—Rom had to be warned.

"Congratulations on your promotion," Kira shot out, "but we'll have to discuss the personnel report some other time."

She tried to slip past him, but he stopped her. "We'll discuss it now," he insisted.

72

Did he know already?

Fiercely, she shook off his grip and snarled, "I don't think so!"

Perhaps he would take it as a signal, as a clue, but she didn't care. She didn't have time for caution and Damar already knew she couldn't stand him.

She rushed out into the corridor and barely possessed the self-control to wait the extra second for the office door to close behind her.

"Kira to Rom! Don't open that hatch!"

"I already did—"

"Get out of there!"

She almost shouted again, but Damar shot out of the office, stepped past her, and signaled to two passing Cardassian guards.

"Intruder alert! Come with me!"

"When we destroyed the processing station, the Dominion suddenly had something to protect— their last storage of ketracel white. We attacked that processing station for two reasons—one, to deprive them of the white, and two, to get them to protect the barge. The Dominion counts on the Jem'Hadar, and therefore they must have white."

"Yes," General Martok agreed, rather uselessly, as he and Sisko stood in the privacy of Martok's quarters on *Rotarran*. "They have made a grave mistake, placing the barge in orbit so near the Argolis Cluster, where they have their precious sensor array."

"I don't think they realized any problem," Sisko said, "luckily for us. They just used the barge because it was already there. I suppose they might've thought Starfleet would notice it if they moved it. A good bet, but not good enough. We've got an edge."

"What kind of edge are you meaning, Captain?"

"A psychological one. The Dominion has suffered a great loss in that processing facility. Now they have to put most of their stock in their storage bank of white. They need the white as much as the Jem'Hadar need it, because the Dominion needs the Jem'Hadar. You know, General, there's a constant threat hanging over the Dominion. The shapeshifters themselves aren't fighters. Neither are the Vorta. They all need the Jem'Hadar to do their heavy lifting for them. The Jem'Hadar haven't really figured that out yet because they're at the mercy of the Vorta and the shapeshifters, who control the ketracel-white supply."

Sisko drew a long breath, tried to relax—more and more rare these days—and to think clearly.

"If the day ever comes," he went on, "when the Jem'Hadar control a major portion of ketracel white, there's the looming chance that they'll turn on the Dominion and negotiate for more power, or even for independence. The Dominion must know that's a possibility."

"Even more possible in this time of war," Martok added, "would be the Federation's control of a portion of white, and therefore Federation control of

Jem'Hadar. That, surely, must frighten the Dominion, and even more the Vorta."

With a musing smile, Sisko agreed. "It'd scare me if I were them. It's very hard to design a creature intelligent enough to fight battles, make choices, repair ships, and plan strategy without also giving it enough independent thought that it might not be completely subservient. The Jem'Hadar are in thrall to the Dominion, but they're independent enough to be turned if somebody else controls the white or if they get control of it themselves. That's our trump card, General . . . I want to make the Dominion think we're trying to capture that storage facility, not just destroy it. If they believe the Federation actually might get a grip on the Jem'Hadar, that'll frighten them more than just a shortage of white. We have to go in and stage some kind of capturing maneuver on that barge, without appearing that we're trying to destroy it. That's the illusion."

Martok frowned. "An illusion that will leave us without the barge."

"No, we won't have the barge. We'll come out of that assault looking like losers. But if the Dominion thinks we're grabbing their last repository of leverage, they're going to pull guard ships off that sensor array. The storage barge loaded with ketracel white will suddenly be a lot more valuable at the immediate moment. I want control over that immediate moment, General."

Still seeming unconvinced, Martok tilted his massive head. "They will not leave the array unprotected, Captain, you know that. We may draw off some of the ships, but hardly all. Perhaps not enough to help Dax."

"I know it's a chance. But if you create a big enough stir, we can keep Dax from having to face an overwhelming force. You said you have the ID information for those ships?"

"Gained at great cost." Martok opened a safe near his bunk and pulled out a spy's gadget—a coded pill about the size of a fingernail infused with information on a chip that could be fed into almost any computer. He immediately handed the pill to Sisko. "The prize of the day. We had to fight them for nearly an hour, then escape with our lives. Two Klingon fighters did not escape at all. For my crew, it was very hard to run away."

Turning the precious pill in his hands, Sisko assured, "You ran for good reason, Martok. Keep the bigger picture in mind."

"I can, but a Klingon crew is an impatient animal with too much pride. How will Dax kill an array of a hundred sensor dishes with one ship?"

Until that question came up, Ben Sisko had been pleased enough with explaining his plan to General Martok in the privacy of the general's own quarters on the Klingon bird of prey he had continued to fly for years despite promotions and senior status. That choice made Sisko admire Martok, and miss the *Defiant*. Guess that was no mystery.

Now for the hard part.

"We came up with a rough plan. It was O'Brien's idea." Sisko dropped into Martok's desk chair. The general was sitting on his bunk, as if he knew that Sisko would not sit there and he wanted him to sit down. Fine, sit. "I'll admit, I don't like it much, but . . . this is war. The sensor array is made up of over a hundred antenna dishes situated on asteroids and planets all over the Argolis system, flanking the cluster itself. To take each one out—"

"Would take a year of ground assault missions," Martok said with a nod.

Sisko shrugged. "Or a hell of a lot of lucky hits from space. We could never get even half of them from space. Our tidy little alternative is to hit the main broadcast station on a planet near the middle of the array. That station controls the hundred individual dishes."

Cranking around to the replicator, Martok keyed up a couple of hot drinks. "How will you do it?"

"We'll pretend to do the insane and impractical obvious thing—attack a bunch of these dishes, take all the potshots we want, while surreptitiously dropping one commando—"

Martok's brows shot up. "One man?"

"Yes, one man, right into the area of the main broadcast station. This man, then, with stealth and brilliance and, I hope, good luck, exacts a singular destructive assault on the station."

"Blows it up."

"Yes, blows it up. Meanwhile, the *Defiant* continues hit-and-running the individual dishes, distracting any ships left defending them and hopefully keeping them from knowing that there's a man infiltrating the source."

"And for us, you and I . . ."

"You and I stage our attack on the ketracel-white barge. We'll try not to take withering losses, General. I'm afraid your crew is going to have to swallow another retreat. The mission isn't to destroy the station—"

"It is rather to attract and distract the Jem'Hadar guarding the Argolis array for as long as possible."

"Yes. We won't even attempt to sneak in. We'll make a lot of noise. Circle and posture long enough to confirm the identity of any ships that show up and hope the numbers match up with the ones on this list. That way, Dax'll only have to deal with the picket ships left behind."

Martok sipped his drink and slowly nodded, designing the whole scheme in his mind. "One question."

Somehow this was a relief for Sisko. He'd tried to think of everything, tried to make this mission something he liked, but no matter what he did or how he twisted mentally, he couldn't enjoy sending the *Defiant* into enemy space by itself, then subdividing one person away from the ship to exact an assault on a planet that probably had enemy troops on the surface. What hadn't he thought of?

"Please," he invited, "ask your question."

"Why can you not just attack the broadcast base from space? Why drop someone in on a suicide mission when you can hit from space?"

This was the thing that hurt most, that made Sisko's stomach kick against the hot drink he clutched. *Suicide* mission.

"Intelligence sent in cloaked probes and have brought back some detailed analyses of how the array works. It must've taken the Dominion months to set up the sensor dishes. Starfleet has figured out that the broadcast base can't be destroyed from outside without triggering independent dishes to run themselves. If the main base shuts down from an outside attack, the dishes take over their own programming. We have to prevent that signal from being sent."

"Wait—this confuses me. If the broadcast base is destroyed, the sensor dishes take over for themselves?"

"Yes, for a certain amount of time, until the main broadcast can be rebuilt, they can run themselves. They'll do that if they're cut off from the broadcast base by an outside strike."

"An *outside* strike. So you mean that your commando can somehow obliterate the base from *inside,* without triggering the dishes to go off and run themselves independently. You need an internal strike. You need this suicide mission."

"That's . . . that's right. The last thing the Dominion wants is for those dishes to fall into enemy hands. We could just as easily use the array against them. If the base is destroyed from outside, the dishes assume the Dominion hasn't yet lost the planet and can take control again. However, if the base is destroyed from inside, the dishes assume the planet is lost, the base is about to fall into enemy hands, and is being controlled from inside. It sends a signal to the dishes that fries them instead of turning them on independently. They'll all self-destruct. But we have to send the right kind of signal to get them to do that."

"So there must be technical wizardry from your commando."

"As Chief O'Brien explains it, the infiltrator has to go inside and adjust the signals to trick the array into thinking it's in enemy hands or that the Jem'Hadar have destroyed the base themselves. Then, all the dishes will self-immolate instead of taking over programming."

"Your commando must land upon this planet and go inside the building, which is likely guarded by many Jem'Hadar soldiers and probably a forcefield and probably mines. He must trigger this destruct signal to a hundred dishes on a hundred asteroids and planets and somehow get out alive by being picked up by the *Defiant*, which will be under attack in space. This is your plan."

An unbidden groan rose in Sisko's throat. His

hands fell into his lap. "That's just about . . . the whole picture."

Martok gazed at him for several seconds. Then he raised his mug.

"Everyone must die sometime," he said, "and the fortunate die in battle. Congratulate your commando for me, Captain. He is on the way to an excellent death."

Miles O'Brien made his way from his cramped quarters aboard *Defiant* to Dax's quarters. They were both off duty, which was almost a silly concept under these conditions, but they had to sleep sometime. And the voyage was long. And sticking to a watch schedule did the crew good. Felt right. Felt ready. One more day to the edge of Argolis, where they would then be awake for days longer. There, they would have to punch through the stormy core of the Argolis Cluster's heart.

The shields were reinforced, but the cluster would take its toll and there might not be enough deflector power to defend against the picket ships which came to fight them. He had held back on the reinforcement. That balance between what they needed now, what they would need for something they could only half measure, and what they would need for a fight they couldn't judge at all—he'd played through all the equations and done his best, but it came down to guessing.

Now he carried a duffel of gear down to Dax's quarters, things that would be necessary for the one-man raid on the broadcast base. He chimed the door, and she instantly called for him to enter, proving that she wasn't asleep.

"Good—you're still up." O'Brien slipped inside with the duffel.

"Can't sleep," Dax told him as she joined him at the small desk. "Are you finished?"

He grimaced. "Oh, bad, bad choice of words."

"Sorry." She smiled at him. "Are you all done mounting our little surprise for the Jem'Hadar?"

With a shrug, he sighed. "We removed six bulkheads and packed sections five, nine, and ten with torpedo caskets, all fully armed, rigged in rapid-fire racks. The racks were the hardest part. Wait'll you see 'em! We're fairly bristling with torpedoes. It's a good thing we reduced the crew complement, or we'd never have gotten all the photons on board. We had to pull out a whole deck of crew quarters!"

"No sense taking anything more than a skeleton crew on a mission like this anyway," Dax commented. She seemed tired, but O'Brien knew it was something else.

"Now I know," he went on, "why it's against regulations to load this many photons onto a ship. One hull breach in those sections, and *foooom*. But they'll fire like crazy when you punch in the sequence. They can't even be aimed, so no sense trying. It's a punching technique, no more and no less."

"One ship against many. We need the edge, regulations or not." Dax opened the duffel he'd put on her desk and looked inside. "Is this the gear for the raid?"

"Right. Specially adjusted tricorder . . . phaser with two power packs . . . five grenades . . . survival kit, hydrator, desalinator, lights . . . and the firecrackers that'll do the job. Ten quantum explosives, and twelve detonators. That's about all one person can carry and move fast."

Dax pawed lightly through the gear, nodding in satisfaction. "It's just right."

"Well, we hope it is," O'Brien said. "That planet is shielded against sensor penetration by some Jem'Hadar satellites, probably to keep us from counting how many Jem'Hadar soldiers are guarding the place on the surface. So, we haven't been able to learn much about the planet or the base's surrounding area, give or take schematics of the mechanical interior of the base itself. The planet, we can't even tell climate very well. We know there are rocks and trees, but otherwise we've got no idea what we're beaming down into."

"What's this blue pack?"

"Compact field jacket. Might get cold at night."

She looked at him. "You anticipating a campout?"

"Have to," he told her. "Can't assume the *Defiant* will be able to double back. We don't know how many picket ships we'll be forced to face down. Might have to stay on the planet for days or weeks. Who knows? Years, maybe, if the war lasts that long."

"Or a lifetime if the Dominion wins," she confirmed and picked up the airtight pack which had the thermal jacket inside. "I take a long torso. This isn't my size."

"Why should it be? I'm the one it's got to fit."

That was it. They locked glares.

"What do you mean, 'you'?" she challenged.

He shrugged and put a possessive hand on the duffel. "Well, who else could possibly go? Sure, most of our engineers could handle the mission if it were a textbook case, but we can't count on that. There's going to be a lot of improvising. If there's a problem, it'll take a senior engineer with some jury-rigging experience. There's nobody better on board than little me."

Dax's black eyes flashed. "Oh, yes, there is. There's little *me.*"

Though he wasn't entirely surprised, O'Brien deliberately stepped back, cocked his hip, tipped his head, and let his jaw drop as if in shock. "You! Now, look—"

Instantly Dax interrupted, "You're not going to argue with your captain, are you, Miles?"

His saucy Irish temper flared. Usually he kept it leashed up, but this was time for a bite.

"Oh, damned right I am! You can't do everything yourself. You're not just Captain Sisko's majordomo anymore, Jadzia. You're not a unit leader. You're a ship's commander on a wide-ranging mission. You're in charge of more than the ground assault, y'know."

"Miles, I'm not sending anybody down into a pit like that on a suicide mission—no, we both know it is. There's no sense coloring the truth, at least not between us."

Her openness moved him so much that his innards clutched. She was trusting him with thoughts she usually kept to herself or reserved for Captain Sisko. He doubted she had ever voiced such reservations even to Worf, whom she would, hopefully, soon marry. And he knew what she meant—dying in space together was one thing, but to just drop a shipmate on a planet, behind enemy lines, where there's almost no chance of a successful pickup . . . pretty distasteful.

She was the captain. What could he do if she insisted on going herself? Orders were still orders, even behind the lines and even going into a mission they might never get out of. In fact orders were more orders than ever, now. He couldn't just flex a muscle and insist. He had to make a good case.

Fortunately, he thought he had one.

Seeing a reflection of himself and her in the little vanity mirror beside the bunk, he straightened his posture a little and wished he'd had time for a haircut. Right now his buff curls looked a bit too boyish. And Jadzia Dax was her flawless, postured self, elegant and queenly in her simple shipboard jumpsuit. Oh, well, he couldn't out-regal her. He'd have to do something else.

"What do you think Captain Sisko felt like, sending us out on this mission without him?"

Apparently surprised by the abrupt change of subject, Dax seemed troubled. "As if his heart had been cut out, I imagine."

"I imagine that too," O'Brien said, "but he did it. He wanted to come, you can bet, but when he was needed to do bigger things, he stayed to do them."

Suddenly Dax turned away from him. Her shoulders flexed and her long black hair, tied at the nape of her neck, rolled between her shoulderblades. "All right, Miles, I know where you're going with that."

She didn't look at him. Somehow that was harder than speaking to her face-to-face.

"I can't run the ship as well as you can," he said, "and you're not an engineering specialist. No matter what kind of image we Starfleeters try to put across, we're not interchangeable. We *can't* do each other's jobs as well as we pretend. You're in command of this mission—the whole mission, not just one part of it. You've got a hard job and I'm glad it's not mine. You've got to choose which people are best to do which tasks. The broadcast base . . . that's mine and you know it."

She still didn't turn to face him. He did empathize with her. In fact he was bothered—her composure didn't crack very often. Usually Dax didn't need anybody's empathy. She always had her ducks in a row, always floated behind somebody else who had bigger problems, providing support and answers and steadiness. But now she was in command. The problems had been shifted onto her narrow shoulders and for the first time since O'Brien could remember, she seemed unsure of herself and deeply troubled.

The sight shook him to his bones.

Jadzia Dax wasn't what she appeared to be on any level. She appeared to be a young woman, subdued and intelligent, accepting of whatever came along. But that was a false image. Really, she was a blend of alien manners of survival, a merging of two life-forms—a young woman and a very old alien. In body, she was young. In mind, she had lived hundreds of years, loved and lost, seen and learned. It was hard most of the time to remember she wasn't human, but she wasn't. To Dax, a human being lived such a short life and was snuffed out so early . . . she had lived hundreds of years among creatures who only lived a few decades. What must they seem like to her? O'Brien knew that, for Dax, sending him to that planet was almost like sending a child to die.

But O'Brien, too, was defending his wife and

children. He knew the Federation was losing. If the Dominion won, humanity would bear the brunt of reprisal as the race that had led the charge. They'd be lucky if the Dominion let them live at all, never mind live well. Chattel slaves had a better idea of the future than he did for his family right now.

"If I get in trouble," he began again, tentatively, "who's best to get me out of there?"

Several seconds went by. She still didn't turn.

"I am . . ."

"If I fail, who's best to launch a second attempt?"

As ridiculous as they both knew that was—there were no second chances in this kind of game—but there was no harm in hope.

She didn't answer. They both knew.

"We're not that sure of what's inside that base, technically speaking."

O'Brien paused. This was all wrong. They were pretending. He had to do better.

"I'm the best to go down there and deal with it, and you're the best to dodge about and pretend to target those dishes. Look, I know what I'm getting into. You needn't . . . you don't have to make any promises you can't keep. Once you drop me, just distract those ships until I can send the destruct signal. You'll know I've done it when the dishes in the array start blowing up. If I don't make it, they just won't blow. Either way, wait as long as you think is right, then use the torpedoes to plow your way out of Argolis." He lowered his voice now, and added, "I understand if you don't come back for me. It's a habitable planet . . . I'll find a way to live."

Live, he knew, contingent upon the big "if" of whether or not he could possibly survive the assault on the broadcast base at all. He knew also, and so did she, that even if he succeeded, the enraged Jem'Hadar certainly would find him.

He knew. They both knew.

"The array has to come down, Dax," he finished. "I've done all I can here. Your job's just starting. So let's each do what we're best at. Go on, now . . . be a captain. Give the right order."

Victory at all costs, victory in spite of all terror, victory however long and hard the road may be; for without victory there is no survival.

Lord Winston Churchill

CHAPTER
6

"THAT'S A suicide maneuver!"

"Only if we get killed."

"Ben!"

"Mind your helm, Charlie. I'm sorry."

Well, that was a lousy answer. Captain Charlie Reynolds easily stayed on his feet despite the pitching and yawing of *Centaur,* which made Ben Sisko tip and grab for balance against the helm where the other captain—now the commodore of this assault team—was standing. *Centaur* was smaller than *Defiant* and the maneuvers were like suction in a wind tunnel as the snarling little ship wheeled tightly before five Jem'Hadar ships in attack formation. Now Sisko had asked Reynolds to turn about—a sanity-straining maneuver while being pursued—

and roll back into that formation and strafe those ships and make them follow off in another direction.

Why?

"Rotarran, veer toward the barge," Sisko called clearly over the bridge noises, *"Traynor,* break toward the cluster and open fire . . . *K'lashm'a,* follow them halfway and break right."

Reynolds watched the action as it was being directed, and knew he was right. This was a good way to get killed while gaining nothing at all. A patchwork task force of five Starfleet and Klingon ships, racing in about as subtle as bulls, staging this assault but not really concentrating on the target. So what were they doing?

"Full burn on all weapons," Sisko went on, as his orders were instantly funneled from *Centaur* to the other task force ships. "Don't save anything . . . *Lyric,* angle ten degrees! Good . . . good . . . broad formation, everyone, stay away from each other . . . good . . ."

Reynolds listened to what Sisko was saying with great curiosity and annoyance as he also fed orders to his own crew, more specific than Sisko's, so the *Centaur* could make its moves at its own most efficient manner. There were subtle differences between styles of ship, different methods of getting each individual vessel to do its personal best.

As Sisko gave orders to the task force ships and Charlie Reynolds gave order after order to his own crew, Reynolds kept glancing and leering and angling at Sisko until he finally started to get reactions out of his old acquaintance. A twinge—was it guilt?—crimped Sisko's eyes as Reynolds divided his attention between Sisko and the action on the screen. Sisko had asked a lot of the *Centaur*'s crew today. A lot of silence, a lot of vagueness, a lot of loaded glares that explained nothing. Go over the border into the Argolis area, stage a losing attack on an orbiting barge with Federation configuration, probably get killed here, but don't ask any questions and *don't* try to destroy the barge or its store of ketracel? Who could figure that?

Even in times of war, such quirkish behavior was a lump to swallow. When men and women went out to fight and die, they needed an idea of what they were fighting and dying for. But the maneuvers Sisko had ordered for *Centaur* and for *Rotarran*—out there somewhere, firing on the barge—were silly actions geared to confuse the linear-minded Jem'Hadar and stall the duration of this battle as long as possible.

"You're just mad at me because I didn't recognize you last time I saw you," Reynolds complained as they dodged between two crossing enemy fighters.

Sisko glanced at him. "My fault. I wasn't wearing my usual ship."

By now, after half an hour of fighting, damage, and casualties, Charlie knew the assault on the barge was half-assed and staged. He knew the other ships' attacks and *Centaur*'s ridiculous maneuvers were going to get them nowhere when it came to capturing that barge. And it was aggravating—Reynolds and his entire crew would happily do something ridiculous if only they had some clue why they were doing it.

"Keep shields moving on all vessels," Sisko ordered to the communications network. "Flash through any anticipated movements to all our ships. Tell Martok to change superior assault position with the *Traynor,* then to *Lyric* after three minutes. Keep the Jem'Hadar from knowing which ship is in charge. I don't want them focusing attention."

"Helm, use your lateral stabilizers more," Reynolds said, pretty much speaking at the same time. "Come on, Randy, you know better than that!"

"Sorry, Charlie."

"Weapons on pinpoint. Aryl, shut down any noncritical systems. Life support on nominal—save whatever we've got. Double shields now, Fitz. We're outmatched four to one. Eyes open. Fire, fire, fire, keep it up, fire as you bear, don't stop—"

"We're burning ourselves out in two rounds," Roger Buick snarled, "and it's a twelve-round match."

Gerrie twisted around from her science panel, still keeping her hands on the board. "They've got another half-dozen ships coming in. At least five, sir."

"From which direction?" Sisko asked.

"Several different directions, sir."

"Pick the tightest cluster and head right at them, full shields—Charlie, you do it."

At the last second, Sisko had remembered he wasn't the captain here, and while Reynolds appreciated that, he still didn't understand such a goofy series of actions. Head at them? Why?

"Track their residual trails," Sisko added, glancing at Gerrie Ruddy. "See where they came from."

Irritated now and feeling as if his uniform were shrinking, Reynolds snapped around to him and demanded, "Why in blazes is *that* important?"

Drenched with perspiration that matted his wispy blond hair, Reynolds finally felt his teeth grate one too many times. He shoved his way through his sweating crew and the cloud of smoke puffing from damaged boards to come to Sisko's side. Ignoring the twisting action on the screen and the ram of incoming shots, he let his crew do the hard stuff, and fixed his eyes on Sisko.

"Okay, flag on the play." He faced Sisko, gathered the shreds of shipboard diplomacy and kept his voice between them. "Assuming Ben Sisko isn't insane, which I doubt, assuming he's not stupid, which I know, then he's got to have a reason for all this silliness. It's pretty clear now we're not here to destroy or even capture that barge."

"But the Jem'Hadar only analyze behavior, not motivations," Sisko told him, "and that means they can be fooled by silly actions."

"Yeah, but there's a shipload of people right here who are risking their lives to be silly and right now it's not going over too great. I know how my people work best—"

"Too many questions, Charlie," Ben Sisko chided as he moved his big shoulders in empathic echo of the dodging ships out there and kept one grip on the edge of the helm.

"Too bad," Reynolds persisted. He took a step closer and folded his arms, flagrantly showing off that he didn't need to hold on to anything to keep his feet under him. "If you won't talk to me, then I'll talk to myself. What could possibly be bigger than destroying most of the ketracel white in this quadrant? Well, it *could* be capturing the ketracel white, but we're not trying to do that very well, are we? I know, I know . . . questions. Okay, I'll just talk and when I'm wrong you tell me. The only thing bigger than the white is that damned wormhole which I wish to hell had never opened up its fat mouth in the first place. The only thing keeping us from taking back DS9 is the fact that we move our fleet and nobody can move a whole fleet without everybody else knowing all about it. Am I getting warm?"

Sisko pressed his lips. "You're giving me a tan."

"We're gonna take on more and more Jem'Hadar ships and still win?" Reynolds plowed on. "Even if all five of our ships strafe that barge, it won't be enough. These aren't assault maneuvers. These are stalling maneuvers. You're buying time. Are we throwing ourselves on a grenade here?"

Sacrificing themselves—that was a noble but distasteful concept and he just wanted to know. Noticing Sisko's unease, Reynolds refused to back off, though he whittled the untimely conversation down to its most simple denominator.

"Why don't you just tell me what you *want?*" he asked.

Stalling on another plane, Sisko heaved a few breaths of frustration, but Reynolds tightened his folded arms and made clear he wasn't moving till he got an answer. Mentally he vibrated the image of a rotting skeleton still standing here ten thousand years from now, waiting for a grunt from a mummified stationmaster.

"All right," the commodore ultimately relented. "I want . . . you're going to hate this."

"I hate it already. Give."

"I want the ID numbers off all the enemy ships that show up here."

"ID numbers," Reynolds repeated, tasting the words. Yes, a nutty answer, but he was suddenly curious now. "For reference or comparison?"

"Both." Sisko reached into his boot and pulled out a little chip, about so big and not very thick, and handed it to him. "There's the list. Line up the numbers, Charlie."

Turning the chip in his fingers, Reynolds narrowed

his eyes. "Mmm . . . both . . . uh-huh . . . hmmm. Okay. All hands, listen up!"

As Sisko smiled at him in spite of the crashing, the banging, the whining, and billows of sparking smoke, Reynolds turned to his overworked crew and waved the smoke away from his eyes.

"Apparently," he began, with a sly glance back at Sisko, "our job is to get the ID information off any Jem'Hadar ship that comes into this area, got it? Use weapons to defend and divert. Don't pump energy into destruction unless you've got a shot nobody in his right mind could refuse. Since none of you losers are in your right minds, none of this should be— Randy, veer right!"

The *Centaur*'s worn deck carpet dropped from beneath their feet as the ship pressed hard to starboard and elevatored upward a few degrees to clear a vicious-looking Jem'Hadar ship that launched from behind a lingering detonation cloud and now took a good shot at them.

The shot missed, but the residual energy wave kicked *Centaur* in the left warp nacelle. Reynolds noticed that Sisko grasped the helm and almost went down on one knee, but Reynolds himself managed to keep both feet under him. He was more familiar with the tugs and pulls of this vessel, and at the moment proud of that.

But that one had been an almost fatal mistake—at the helm Randy Lang had been looking at Reynolds instead of the screen. Only for an instant, but that one mistake had almost gotten them killed.

Randy's face was flushed with shock of that lesson and now his eyes were fixed on the screen. "Where'd that bastard come from?" he gasped.

"Two more new ones coming in from someplace!" Roger Buick called over the scream of compensators in the engineering trunks. He was juggling both navigation and weapons—then again, who needed to navigate this kind of nonsense?

"Evasive," Reynolds ordered, "but keep tight. Roger, get those numbers! Gerrie, feed this into the computer!" He tossed the little nugget with the list of ship identification up to the science deck, where his science officer grabbed it.

"You've gotta be kidding," Science Officer Geraldine Ruddy grumbled, but she shoved the pill into an all-purpose fitting and worked her sensors, scanning and focusing and pinpointing like crazy.

"Buick," Sisko interrupted, "if you target their engine exhaust ports, instead of their drive systems, and fuse them shut, they'll have to fall back for a few minutes. All we have to do is disable them. Don't waste time trying to go for the kill."

"Understood, sir," Buick responded tightly, though he actually glanced at Sisko as if to remind himself he was taking orders from both his captain and his commodore.

For a brief instant Reynolds let himself be grateful

to Sisko for bothering to learn the names of the *Centaur*'s bridge crew.

More rightly, his words to Buick had been a suggestion, not an order, that could be countermanded by Reynolds if the captain saw some flaw the brilliant commodore hadn't thought of.

"What's the *Rotarran*'s position?" Sisko asked, possibly a means of reminding both this crew and himself that he wasn't trying to overshadow their own captain and that he knew his job here. Reynolds was grateful again, though not inclined to thank Sisko just yet for a darned thing.

"They're on the underside of the barge, sir," Ensign Aryl reported. "Strafing aft, with three Jem'Hadar on them!"

"Maintain surveillance. If they get into trouble, we'll have to veer back and help."

"We're all in trouble," Reynolds muttered. "Two ships against all these—"

"Try to keep track of which ones were here when we arrived and which are just showing up," Sisko said. "Go after the IDs on the new ships and compare them to the IDs on the list I gave you."

Reynolds tried to control his expression, but a sneer popped out anyway; IDs off Jem'Hadar ships rushing by at high impulse, shooting the whole time. Yeah. As if it were that easy to read the encoded Jem'Hadar markings.

"I'll get the numbers for you," he muttered, pressing forward with both hands on Roger Buick's thick shoulders. "After this is over, you're gonna tell me all about it."

Ben Sisko narrowed his black eyes and in the midst of rocking and rolling, stirred up a snakelike smile.

"That's a deal, Charlie," he said. "That's the best deal I've ever made."

CHAPTER

7

Rough ride. Damned rough ride through that cluster. The ship had almost melted in the heavy radiation and storms, but the double shielding brought them through. If any were left to get back again . . . that remained to be seen.

For now, and possibly for always, it was no longer Miles O'Brien's problem. He had drilled and redrilled the engineers on the *Defiant* to deal with any problems he could wildly imagine to keep the ship from peeling apart, but he couldn't possibly anticipate their actions after facing down a bunch of Jem'Hadar ships and whatever damage they might also have to deal with. He stopped short of calculating the ship's chances of ever seeing Federation space again. That was too much for a man's soul to hold.

A strange fatalism overtook him as he felt himself rematerialize and knew he was on the planet where the broadcast station was nestled. In fact, as his eyes cleared, he saw that he was inside a vestibule of some sort, a constructed tunnel.

"Good shooting, Dax," he muttered. Best aim with transporters he'd seen in a year, and they'd dropped him off without even reducing speed. He was warmed by Dax's insistence to work the transporter herself, even in the midst of onrushing Jem'Hadar picket ships.

They'd counted six ships racing in from the outlying regions of the Argolis system. So that fight was on. And he was down here.

And after days of silent running, minutes suddenly counted. He had to send the destruct signal to those dishes, so they would blow themselves up and Dax would see it. Then he had to take out this whole facility with his little concussion-incendiaries.

"Or die trying."

Tricorder clicked in his hands, scanning the immediate area. Four . . . seven . . . at least ten Jem'Hadar readings close by. But he didn't see any of them.

So far, so good—no intruder alert alarms going off. Nothing was reading his presence, at least not yet. That gave him a few seconds.

Slipping his pack off his shoulder, he held it in front of him at the ready, kept his hand on his phaser without taking the weapon off his belt yet, because he would need his hands, and stood up straight. Here in the shadows, if he didn't crouch, he might look like just another Jem'Hadar to someone looking this way. Trying to appear confident and in place to any peripheral glances, he strode into the broadcast complex.

The base comprised three buildings, one main and two auxiliary. He was at what they guessed was the back door of the main building. Ahead of him was a series of cubiclelike openings that actually were corridors. The walls of each corridor were encrusted with technology—panels, monitors, access links, and everything necessary to run the hundred sensor dishes in the systemwide array.

With his skin crawling, O'Brien strode into the dim complex, doing his best Jem'Hadar clunky stagger. Keeping to the shadows, he held the short duffel up against his chest to hide the tricorder.

Emissions . . . long-range emissions . . . there! Perfect . . . he knew just what to look for . . . now he just had to track the signals . . . Luckily most of the Jem'Hadar technology wasn't a mystery. The Vorta were secretive, but not very technical. The Jem'Hadar they ordered around were technical, but not very imaginative. They didn't understand about tricks and secrets, decoys and false leads. They knew what worked and why, and they just made things work.

That left tiny openings for O'Brien and others

who were learning that cleverness and trickery were things the Jem'Hadar didn't understand.

A hard chill ran up his spine as a movement to his left attracted his attention. Deep in the dim corridor, three Jem'Hadar soldiers crossed his path.

Not moving too fast, he turned sharply and stepped into one of the cubicle openings that led to the computer and mechanical panels running the complex. If those soldiers came this way, they would be able to see right in here, and this place had a worklight shining in it. There was no place to hide— and the corridor was a dead end.

Frustration set in. The tricorder provided him with a neat map to the array signal source. Three cubicles down to his right, then a hundred meters northeast. That would lead into the center of this building, the way it was situated in the landscape.

Cold in here . . . the hastily poured concrete floor was uneven and grainy and sucked the heat out of his body right through the soles of his boots and into the ground. In spite of that he was sweating and his black-on-black infiltration suit was clammy against his arms and chest. Why hadn't he just brought a Jem'Hadar Halloween mask? He could've walked around here all day.

Funny what they hadn't thought of. Wouldn't have been so hard—

Footsteps!

He pressed his back against the nearest wall.

Would they just walk by? Or would they look in here? No shadow, no desk, nothing to hide behind. O'Brien flattened himself as much as possible, held the duffel bag behind his thigh, and leveled his phaser at the cubicle opening.

The mutter of Jem'Hadar voices gnawed at him. He couldn't hear what they were saying, couldn't quite make out the words—more shuffling footsteps . . . were they armed?

Probably.

He was ready . . . he had a specially programmed computer cartridge that would send the destruct signal to the dishes. It was all ready, right here in his duffel's side pocket. All he had to do was get to the broadcast point and plug it in, then ignite the signal. The whole thing would only take seven to ten seconds.

If he could just get there.

The Jem'Hadar shuffling was right here now, just opposite the entry to this cubicle. Were they passing by? Please, pass by, pass by . . .

His phaser was set to kill. No sense taking chances. If only he could've set it on wide-angle— but that would be too risky in here. Too much mechanics that could shatter and blow back on O'Brien himself. There were places where a phaser could be wide-ranged and places where it shouldn't be.

They were here—he could hear them muttering,

much closer now—only steps away. If only it weren't so bright here!

The footsteps began to fade. Were they leaving? Going outside, maybe? That would be so—

Then a face appeared beside him, a horny face like an open jawbone. One of the Jem'Hadar!

The soldier strode into the cubicle and reached for a panel, then caught O'Brien in the corner of his eye and swung around, gaping at the intrusion. The soldier opened his mouth to call the others, but O'Brien clutched the phaser.

Unfortunately, the phaser did the soldier's screaming for him. The soldier was blasted backward to crash his heavy body into the panel behind him, smashing several lighted readouts. By the time the sparks rose, that soldier was dead and sizzling against the lower trunk.

O'Brien didn't wait for the others. He ducked out of the cubicle with the phaser announcing him the whole way. Two . . . three down! Three dead Jem'Hadar and no more in sight right now. Had they alerted anybody when his phaser first went off?

The hall was cleared now, but he didn't fool himself into thinking that was the end of it. Clutching his duffel under one arm and holding the phaser out before him, he broke into a full-out run in the direction the tricorder had indicated.

The place where the signal computer was housed—would it be defensible? Would he have seven to ten seconds before they came in and killed him? Could he hold them off that long?

That would mean he only got half the job done. Destroying the dishes would give the Federation a little time, but wouldn't cripple the Dominion for long. This base had to come down—and he was going to die in here before he could make that happen. If only he could contact Dax, tell her to blast the complex from space *after* the dishes blew up . . . he should've told her to do that anyway.

Irritated that they hadn't just accepted that this was a suicide mission and dealt with it as such, he plowed his way past crates of equipment and locked cabinets, blasting the cabinets and crates into shards as he ran past them. The crates blew to smithereens, and the padlocked cabinets cracked open like eggs, spilling precious ketracel white in a hundred little tubes that crashed to the ground and left a spreading slick of milky liquid behind him.

A loud bell-ringing alarm went off all around him, almost driving him down with sheer loudness. What had triggered it? Those soldiers must've hit a switch or an alert before he came out and blew them away. Couldn't exactly blame them. It was part of the game.

He ran like a fool straight down the middle of the corridor, with such plowboy willfulness that he ran right past the cubicle opening to the corridor with the broadcast signal housing. Twenty paces down, he skidded around, almost slipping in the slick of ketracel white, then skidded his way back to the right opening—

And now he could see at least a dozen troops of Jem'Hadar surging into the dimness from the wedge of light from the main tunnel!

They opened fire as soon as they saw him, but he ducked and zigzagged out of their sights. Their distruptor fire tore apart the walls around him and clawed at the floor beneath his running feet, but finally he zagged hard to his left and plunged into the cubicle. Was it the right one this time? If not, it was all over. There was no going back.

The wall just ahead of him opened up with disruptor fire, cracking as if an earthquake had gouged it, and half the stony wall caved in on him. He tried to jump over it, but tripped and went down hard on the point of his left knee. Grimacing in pain, he forced himself to continue without missing a step.

Slinging the duffel's strap over his shoulder, still firing back the way he'd come with one hand, he used the other hand to dig into the side pocket and pull out the computer cartridge that meant everything. Well, half of everything.

He stopped shooting and concentrated on ducking the shots from the Jem'Hadar who were chasing him. He was faster, a pretty good sprinter in his day, and put half the complex behind him while the Jem'Hadar fell behind. Every pace drove a stab of pain from his knee up to his pelvis. If he hadn't fallen he might've been able to run even faster, but

there was no getting that back. Seconds, he needed
seconds . . .

There it was! He recognized the alien computer
broadcast-signal access as if he'd designed it himself! It was so obvious in its purpose it might as well
have been marked "HERE!"

Ducking behind a transverse wall, he turned and
opened fire in a blanketing manner that forced the
pursuing Jem'Hadar to stop chasing him and take
cover. Streaks of disruptor energy bit into the thing
he was hiding behind and took off the top half of it.
Another shot like that, and he would be completely
exposed.

He fired wildly a few more times, then swung
to the computer terminal and searched for the
card insert. There had to be something here—the
Jem'Hadar had built all their equipment to be
compatible with whatever they might find in the
Alpha Quadrant. That was their idea of being ready
to take over whatever they found.

Today, their prudence was in O'Brien's favor. The
access was in an abnormal place, but he did find it
and the cartridge fit just right. The computer came
to life and started asking for instructions. He took
the time for two more blanketing shots, then tapped
in an override order. He gave it the answer—*You've
fallen into enemy hands. Detonate all dishes.*

The computer distilled his order, took it as an
enemy takeover of the base, and started sending
destruct signals to the dishes far away in space.

"I hope," he muttered. "I hope that's what you're doing. No second chances . . . come on, give me confirmation . . ."

But none came. He had no way to know if the signal had actually been sent. It had been processed, but had it been segmented and broadcast to the dishes? Were they blowing up now? Was Dax seeing them sparkle in deep space as she fought off the Jem'Hadar pickets?

Or was there nothing? Was space still dark and hopeless? Did she think he was already dead? That he'd failed?

Out of time, he swung around on his raging knee and kept low, hiding behind what was left of the jagged wall. There was dust in his eyes and mouth as he tried to see down the dim aisle. There they were! A dozen Jem'Hadar peeking out at him, their disruptors raised toward him.

Well, at least he could take a few of them down with him.

No, there was more he could do! He could set a couple of those incendiary charges and at least blow up part of this computer rack. If he couldn't take out the whole building, at least he could mess it up a little!

Clutching for the duffel bag, he dragged it to his side and tried to dig through it, but his fingers were numb. Why weren't his fingers moving?

A shuffle down the aisle snapped his attention back to the Jem'Hadar. They were coming!

Quickly O'Brien peeked out to get aim, trained his phaser on the clutch of white-faced soldiers lumbering toward him, and squeezed the trigger.

Nothing happened.

He spat an oath and twisted the readjustment on the phaser. Still nothing! His phaser had shut down!

And they were coming!

The power pack still read charged—what was wrong with it?

He hooked the duffel bag on his numb arm and stumbled over the pile of rubble, heading northeast again, but he didn't make it ten steps before the low ceiling over his head blew to spatters and drove him down to the scratchy concrete floor. The concrete ripped his clothing and chewed at his skin. His leg was throbbing and weak now, his right arm still numb. Behind him he heard the shiff-shiff of Jem'Hadar boots scratching through the rubble.

He was done for. Half a job, and he was finished. The muscles in his back cramped in anticipation of disruptor fire. What would it feel like to die that way?

BOOM!

A deafening roar shocked him to a stupor and he covered his head with his arms.

Click—BOOM!

What the hell was that?

"Get up! On your feet!"

Click—BOOM!

Gathering his splattered wits, O'Brien twisted and

looked up into a cloud of dust and smoke. There, standing above him, looking back the way he'd come, was a man. Nobody special, just a man, except that from this angle the newcomer seemed like a redwood tree at dawn, rising out of the rocks and rubble to tower over the insect at its base.

"Get up!"

BOOM!

Some kind of concussion rifle stretched from the man's grip and spat black fire at the scattering Jem'Hadar.

O'Brien twisted over on his back and looked at the enemy troops. The nearest Jem'Hadar's head was cracked in two and opened up like a melon hit with a hammer. Exposed brains were blown free and splattered the wall with blue matter and white liquid. The body lay less than a meter away from him. That was close.

Down the aisle were more slaughtered Jem'Hadar, each with a hole in him the size of a worklight. Guts and white spilled down the fronts of their smashed torsos. And of those left from the original dozen pursuers, disruptors flew out of their hands and their ranks opened before O'Brien and the intruder like petals flying off an old rose in high wind. In puddles of gore the Jem'Hadar hit the walls, leaving streaks of guts and shattered bone as they slid to the cold floor.

The man called over the noise of his own weapon. "Can you shoot?"

O'Brien shook himself and forced his voice out, "My phaser's jammed or—or seized!"

"Your what is what?"

Desperately he plucked at the inert weapon's setting panel. "This place has some kind of energy damping field! I can't shoot!"

"That's all right," the intruder said. "I *can.*"

And he started walking forward, down the aisle O'Brien had just marathoned, dealing death faster than the Jem'Hadar could even take aim. O'Brien scratched to his feet, slung the duffel's strap back over his shoulder, and stumbled after him.

Suddenly the man shoved his heavy weapon into O'Brien's hand, along with some kind of metal clip, and shouted, "Reload this!"

While O'Brien fumbled with the rifle-type weapon, the man yanked a handheld weapon out of his vest and kept shooting, hardly missing a second.

BAM! BAM!

That hand weapon had a different tenor of report but did a terrible thing to the faces of the oncoming Jem'Hadar.

"Come on!" the man called back to O'Brien. "Follow me!"

CHAPTER 8

"More angle! Are the torpedo racks on line?"

"Ready to fire when you are. If just one of those jams on the slide-out, they'll chain-ignite."

"I know. Nog, fire phasers!"

"Rigging a ship with something this dangerous is a court-martial offense, you know, Captain."

"Let's hope we're all alive to be court-martialed, Julian. Lieutenant Haj, continue evasive. Don't let them work our stern. Starboard, faster! Julian, take over the sensors. Keep focused on those dishes. Let me know as soon as you see anything."

Jadzia Dax was out of the command chair, working the Ops and engineering stations herself. Everybody on board was doing two jobs, except that she was also the commanding officer and that meant she was doing a lot more than two jobs.

They were in a hot chase with five Jem'Hadar vessels on their tail. Since dropping off O'Brien they had raced around the system in a flurry of uncoordinated hits, taking potshots at various sensor dishes and even managing to take out a handful of them, but such maneuvers would never make a dent in the hundred units out there. All they had to do was make the Jem'Hadar believe they were after the dishes. O'Brien only needed a few minutes . . . if he were still alive.

"Fire!" Dax called again when the fourth enemy ship tried to take their beam. "Don't let them get in front of us!"

"I'm trying," Nog ground out.

"Nog, take over the Ops! I'll take tactical and weapons."

"Good!"

They switched positions, and that cut out the rigmarole of Dax having to handle two consoles and also watch the enemy ships and also give specific firing orders. Now she could fire at will and cut seconds off the process of keeping alive.

"Dax!"

Bashir was calling, but Dax didn't pay attention to him. There were two ships in range . . . if she could only hit their weapons magazines—

"Dax!" Bashir shouted louder. "Sensors indicate wide-range full-spectrum meltdown in the dish units! Miles did it! He did it! The dishes are blowing up all over the system!"

Through the plasma smoke, she cast him a glowing smile. "Did we ever have a doubt?"

Sheeted in sweat, Bashir was too frightened to return the smile. "Well, actually, yes!"

She turned back to her weapons, wishing she could take the time to look out into space, see the sparkle of detonations from here to eternity. "Haj, lay in a course for the cluster!"

She continued firing, and though *Defiant* sustained ghastly damage in most sections, she managed to detonate any critical incomings and thus protect the sections where the torpedoes were tightly packed; and at the same time she took out three more Jem'Hadar ships. Now they were being pursued by two ships.

"Good shooting!" Bashir gagged, then coughed on the streaming gases erupting from the shattered bridge consoles. "A few more minutes and we won't even be able to breathe in here. Dax? Did you hear me?"

"I heard you. Do what you can about it. Get us masks if you have to."

"Understood! Did you say we're heading for the cluster?" Bashir left his post and stumbled across the shattered deck to her side. "We're not leaving him . . . we're not, are we?"

Her hands cold, she fired the stern phasers again and again. "Those are our orders."

"You're not serious . . ." Even his whisper was like a gong in her ear. "Did he know that?"

"I was supposed to be the one to go," she told him. "I was the only one who knew. I was under command restriction. It's too dangerous to go back for one person. We owe the Federation the opportunity to use this ship again. That means leaving right now."

"Dax," he protested, but he apparently couldn't think of any way to make one man's life worth more than an entire battleship in the middle of a war.

Dax gave him a sorry glance. "We're supposed to use those photon torpedoes to plow our way back into the cluster and clear out of here."

He gripped her tactical console. "Is it worth one pass? An emergency beam-out?"

"We can't slow down enough to pick up just one person. We won't be able to focus the beam that well."

"Listen," Bashir gasped, "I can isolate his combadge signal and we can do a wide-scan transporter beam. It's risky and we might pick up a couple of Jem'Hadar along with him, but at least we can try. You're not leaving without at least trying to get Miles back . . . you wouldn't do that, would you?"

She hit the firing button again, and behind them another Jem'Hadar ship splintered and spun out of control. "No, I'm not leaving without at least trying."

Julian seemed suddenly weak. He pressed his hands on the edge of her console. "Thank God . . ."

"Get back to your post."

"Thank you—"

"Go on. Haj, evasive subport, ten degrees!"

"Captain!" Ensign Nog peered through the gout of smoke, before anyone could move at all. "Ten more Jem'Hadar ships just appeared on our forward screens! They're blocking our way!"

Bashir swung around, obviously frightened that Dax would change her mind. Ten ships, blocking the way between them and O'Brien—

Just then a hard hit from aft blew half the helm console away at the deck level. The flash of electrical impact drove Lieutenant Haj straight backward to crash to the deck with his legs virtually on fire.

"Julian," Dax called, "take over the conn station!"

His complexion dusky with fear, Bashir rushed to the helm and put his hands on the snapping controls. Dax was worried—asking him to steer in these conditions was a risk. He knew the basics, but he was no combat pilot.

"Just head directly into those oncoming ships, Julian," she told him in her steadiest voice.

"Directly into him? No evasive?"

"No evasive." Dax twisted around briefly. "All right, everyone, this is it! Nog, ready all torpedo racks!"

"All racks armed and ready!"

"Wait until they're in range . . . closer . . . closer . . . let's plow our way through! All torpedoes, rapid-fire!"

Blast after blast blew Jem'Hadar soldiers out of their way. O'Brien limped behind the lanky and dangerous stranger.

"Why aren't you shooting?" the man cast back.

"Oh—don't know. Guess I should . . ."

Fumbling with the weapon, he did a quicky diagnostic and figured out where the clip went, clapped it into place, turned the wide-mouthed barrel forward toward one of the Jem'Hadar, and pulled the trigger.

Click—BOOM!

And O'Brien was suddenly flat on his backside in the rubble.

He stared at the weapon in his aching arms. "Well, what the hell . . ."

"Get up, keep moving! Follow me! Keep shooting, now."

He crawled up at the urging of the other man, whose voice was unremitting and gave him strength with its confidence.

The weapon was warm in his hands. What a kick this monster had!

With a modicum of experience now, he aimed and fired again. *BOOM!*

He stayed on his feet this time, but the weapon bucked up in his arms and hit him in the nose. Well, he killed a Jem'Hadar. Not the one he'd been aiming at, but a score was a score.

The other man, though, shattered his way through the storming troops, pausing every few steps to stand, brace-legged like some kind of Texas Ranger, firing again and again in a withering barrage. Together they boomed and bammed their way haltingly forward. O'Brien was astonished at the reaction of the Jem'Hadar who could still move. They were running! The enemy soldiers were running away! Disruptor fire had all but suspended, and the soldiers were ducking down the corridors and hobbling in a Jem'Hadar version of rushing.

A wedge of golden brightness crossed O'Brien's eyes and made him squint. Daylight!

No, not exactly daylight, but a setting sun angling straight down the entry tunnel.

"Go out first," the Texas Ranger ordered, and turned to face the inside of the complex while O'Brien did as he was told and hustled down the tunnel.

"Aren't you coming?" he called back over his shoulder.

"In a minute."

Behind him as he ran, he heard the relentless *BAM BAM BAM* of that iron hand weapon. His own arms trembled from the adrenaline rush and the lingering kick of the weapon he was still carrying.

He broke out into the lowering sunlight, hesitated a moment, then angled toward the nearest stand of rocks and high ground. There were trees up there, bushes, places to hide.

But he'd left that man inside—he could still hear the bang of that handgun, so his friend was alive, at least. O'Brien was about to double back and shout for the other man to get out now, when suddenly his companion jogged out of the tunnel and ran to meet him, taking O'Brien's arm and pulling him up the steep escarpment.

"They'll be flocking here any minute," the man said, "but they don't know how to search very well. I know where we can hide. This way."

They climbed almost straight up, except that Texas knew the rocks so well that he led O'Brien up a craggy natural stairway that twisted and jabbed into the rock formations, negotiating the almost invisible path with the skill of someone who had grown up here. Must be a native of the planet, O'Brien's foggy mind decided.

His chest thudded and constricted—atmosphere must be a little thinner here than he was used to.

"High enough," his companion finally allowed.

O'Brien slid to his knees, shuddering. His eyes fogged over and he gratefully closed them, then sank sideways and collapsed against a rock. Were the Jem'Hadar following? It didn't matter. He couldn't run or climb anymore . . . his knee throbbed furiously. His right arm was numb. He had to rest, just for a minute.

A careful grip took him by one arm and pulled

him to a sitting position. Dazed, he shook his head—what a mistake—and blinked his eyes.

They were wedged into the rocky terrain under a shading clutch of trees and it was almost dark. Enough light remained in the gray sky that he blinked up into the eyes of a pale-skinned man with fairly ordinary eyes and shoulder-length hair the color of the dirt under them.

"You all right?" his new friend asked. He set O'Brien upright and leaned him against an angled rock slab.

O'Brien shook his head—he could barely hear the man's voice. He spat out a crumb of concrete and garbled, "Bedamned . . . phaser . . . neutralized on me!"

Texas held up his own weapon, a harsh-looking ironbound antique rifle with a stumpy body and a wide-mouthed barrel. It looked as if it came out of some amalgamated version of Earth's 1800s. O'Brien had seen pictures of old-style guns, but this one he didn't recognize specifically.

But what a noise it had made! He'd never heard a concussion weapon go off in real life. On the holo-deck, sure, but the automatic program muted any potentially damaging element, and that included noise. This was . . . this was loud!

"Nice shootin', Tex," he drawled as he appreciated the heavy gun and its owner.

"Tex?"

"It's your new nickname."

"Oh." The man sat down beside him and plucked at O'Brien's torn sleeve. "Shoulder's bleeding, did you know that?"

"Ah . . . right. Must've been why my fingers went numb."

"Who are you?"

"What's that? Oh, sorry—somebody's beating my eardrum. I'm Chief Engineer Miles O'Brien, Starfleet, United Federation of Planets."

"Federation," the man repeated. "Been a long time since I heard that word." Then he tipped his head back the way they'd come. "So we're at war?"

"No doubt. What's your name?"

"I'm Cregger Lor Mowlanish Dor Crixa Tel."

"Ah . . . mind if I just keep calling you 'Tex'?"

"Fine with me. What should I call you?"

"Miles. That's some weapon. It drove those soldiers back ten feet each and left a mighty hole. Where'd you get it?"

"We use these to defend our ranches and herds."

O'Brien glanced down into the valley, but saw neither of those. "You live on this planet?"

"Yes," Tex told him. "Lived just fine, until the shellheads came."

Sympathizing, O'Brien understood. "That's not much against phasers."

Tex shook his head, then brushed crumbling dust out of his hair. "Phasers didn't do you a lot of good just now."

With a grunt of empathy, O'Brien said, "You're right about that. Guess you got a shock, didn't you, when the Dominion dropped by?"

"Overnight," Tex confirmed, "they were here, blasting away."

O'Brien held up his phaser. "They had some kind of damping field in there that shut mine down. I should've expected they'd be ready."

Tex leaned back and held up his own enormous boomer. "Can't shut this down."

"No, I suppose not! Just a simple chemical reaction . . . expanding gases propelling a heavy little weight at incredible speed! No way to short *that* out, for sure! The only way to absorb the energy is into the chest of a Jem'Hadar. And, of course, they wouldn't know how to fight this! They're just programmed drones, raised in tubes and made to fight in space with energy weapons. They've got no sense of history, no idea of chemistry, and they're completely unprepared for a hot, fast pellet that blows their heads off! Why didn't I think of that?"

Realizing he was raving a bit, he paused and regarded Tex in the fading light.

"You . . . have a family here?" he asked.

Tex peered over a rock, making sure they weren't being tracked. "So tell me about the war."

"They're trying to take over the whole quadrant."

"Let 'em try." He patted his boomer.

"Why did you get me out?" O'Brien asked.

"Because they were shooting at you. We've been hiding out, waiting for a chance to fight back, but we didn't know how to hurt them most. Then I saw you." He smiled and muttered, "I've been wanting to do that for months. I should've thought to bring a couple of my friends. We could've gotten them all."

Exhausted, O'Brien shook his head. "I've teamed up with John Wayne . . . how many people are in this colony?"

Tex shrugged. "I don't know, exactly. We never thought about it much until they showed up. They haven't even asked us anything. They just came here and started building that complex."

"They didn't hurt your people?"

"They shuffled most of the men and children into camps, then put the women under house arrest and forced them to do the cooking and cleaning for the men and kids in the camps."

"Pretty damned effective."

"Some of us were in the mountains when they came. Me, some of my friends . . . we hid out all this time. They kept looking, but they never found us."

"They're bred for life in space. Bit awkward anyplace else."

"We noticed that. Until today, they didn't know we'd been missed."

"Oh . . . sorry . . . I blew your cover."

"It's all right," Tex said. "We've been planning to move against them. We just weren't sure where to start or what to do. We didn't know how we could

hurt them most. Can you tell me what those buildings do?"

"That's a broadcast complex. It maintains a whole
range of scanning posts in space that tell them where
our ships are and what strengths we've got. Except,
I'm hoping I just spat out a signal that blew up the
dishes before it could flash-transmit a . . . oh, never
mind that part. The second half of my job was to
blow up the base. Unfortunately, I wasn't sneaky
enough. I didn't even get confirmation that the
dishes went to self-destruct mode. Didn't have
time . . . guess I'll just have to hope they did . . . if I
blow up that base without the dishes going first, the
whole mission's worthless."

"You have no way to know?"

"None at all."

"Then do your best with what's here. What've you
got in that bag?"

"Enough explosives to wipe that complex off your
planet. Problem is, they're chain-reaction incendiar-
ies. They have to be planted inside, and now I'm
outside. I've got to get back in there!"

"Why? If you blew up the dishes—"

"If I don't demolish the base," O'Brien explained
again patiently, "all they have to do is replace the
dishes. This complex is the important part."

Pressing a dry cloth to the wound in O'Brien's
shoulder, Tex nodded slowly. "Bad wound."

"I can't feel it much."

"You will."

"Oh . . . yes."

"You want to get back inside?"

O'Brien snapped a glare at him. "Can you get me in? How?"

"Know what mines are?"

"I certainly do!"

"Those shellheads, they don't realize they built their complex right on top of a network of our mines. They never even looked."

A shock of relief and hope drenched O'Brien beneath his sweat-damp suit. "Would you think it was odd if I shook your hand till it fell off, man!"

His sudden companion smiled, then spat out a bit of the wreckage they'd just caused. "How soon do you want to go, Miles?"

Reinvigorated, O'Brien swung around onto his knees and peered over the crest and down at the complex, at flocks of Jem'Hadar who were combing the grounds. "Right now! While they're all out patrolling around and looking for us here. My ship's dodging around space, giving us time. Let's not waste it."

Grinning broadly, Tex brushed back a lock of his dust-brown hair. "Your weapons or mine?"

Enheartened such as he never imagined he would be by today's story, Miles O'Brien clapped his new friend on the shoulder, ignored the puff of dust the gesture raised, and shouldered the wonderful, dependable concussive weapon that had saved his life.

"Tex," he said, "let's go turn that place to taffy!"

In one of the most dangerous maneuvers Dax had ever seen aboard a ship, the *Defiant* began freely spewing photon torpedoes, plowing the way before her with machine-gun deadly force. The ten Jem'Hadar ships before them were riddled with explosions in such rapid succession that they never even had time to angle away from the head-on collision.

The torpedoes spilled off their racks and into the firing chambers and self-launched furiously, faster than anyone could've manually fired them. Dax squinted with tensions—if even one jammed, the explosion would be right here, right now, and it would light up the solar system.

"Approaching the planet," Bashir tensely reported.

"Just graze past it, Julian, don't reduce speed."

"Are you working the sensors yourself? Are you scanning for him?"

"Yes, just steer the ship. Transporter chamber, this is the captain. Ensign Morrison, are you standing by?"

"Yes, Captain, I'm ready when you are."

"This is it, kiddo, you get to prove why you graduated top of your class in transporter technology."

"I'm ready."

"Stand by . . ."

Closer, closer, the *Defiant* blasted right through the spinning remains and splinters of the Jem'Hadar ships they'd blown out of the way.

"Nog, take over what's left of the phasers and maintain fire on the two ships chasing us."

"Captain, they're veering off! They saw what we did to their pals!"

"Good riddance. Pilot us two degrees closer, Julian."

"Two degrees . . . aye."

"Come on, Chief, where are you?" Dax leered at her scanners, searching for the one tiny blip on a whole planet. Dax hoped she sounded more in control to the crew than she sounded to herself. But there was only one chance at this. They'd come swooping in like an albatross with hawks on its tail, trying to isolate the single Starfleet combadge blip in that whole planetary region.

"I've got him! He's there!"

Her own voice surprised her.

"Morrison, energize! Right now, right now!"

Now she had to wait. A deck below, the transporter specialist was beaming up the life-form attached to that combadge, and any other life-forms within five meters of him.

She couldn't shake the feeling that they might be beaming up a corpse.

"I'll take over the helm, Julian," she said on a whim. "You go down there and check."

Bashir's eyes flashed with hope and worry. "Thank you," he gasped, and he rushed off the bridge. Dax took over the helm and punched the comm. "Ensign Richardson to the bridge. I need you for the helm. And find somebody with experience and bring them with you for tactical and scanners."

"Richardson, aye. On my way, Captain."

Had O'Brien detonated the broadcast base? Yes, all the dishes had chain-detonated. If the base weren't destroyed too, the Jem'Hadar could reestablish the sensor array in a couple of weeks.

And the ship and crew weren't exactly out of hot water yet. Shredding her orders, she had doubled back for O'Brien on the thin chance that he had survived a one-man assault on an enemy-packed installation. Oh, well, why not?

Had the transport process finished?

No time to wait. If they didn't have him by now, it was all over. Ensign Richardson and a new lieutenant whose name she couldn't remember right now appeared on the bridge and Dax was able to leave the helm. She wanted to keep steering, but she knew that if she was doing that job, she wasn't doing her job—command.

"Full impulse," she ordered. "Prepare for warp speed. Head directly back into the core of the cluster."

"Understood," Richardson said, without bothering to repeat the details.

On the screens all around the command area,

various visions played—the planet falling away astern of them, the churning Argolis Cluster which they would have to survive a second time when once had been enough.

"Phaser banks are nearly exhausted," Nog reported.

"Knew that was coming," Dax muttered, but she was distracted by the hiss of the door panel and turned to look. "With any luck, we won't need them. How many of the torpedoes did we fire?"

"Every last one of them."

"That's how it was supposed to work."

Nog sighed roughly. "It worked, all right."

Suddenly Julian Bashir piled out of the lift, his greasy, dirty, sweaty face bright with a smile. "We got him!"

On closer look, Dax saw O'Brien limping out of the lift, with Bashir's attentive support.

"Chief—" she gasped. "You'll be ashamed of me when you find out how much I had bet against you!"

"S'all right," O'Brien drawled as Bashir led him to her. "I can send the kids to college with the winnings I get from betting against myself."

"Well? Give me a report!"

"Oh, mission accomplished. It took two assaults, but we set all the grenades and they behaved like champs. The whole base is shattered. Did the dishes go up?"

"Just like fireworks."

O'Brien paled with relief and pressed a supportive

hand on the command chair. Apparently he really hadn't known until now whether he completely succeeded.

"Are you all right, Miles?" Bashir asked. "Look at your shoulder—"

"It's all yours now, Julian," the chief told him. "Oh, Dax, there's one thing. Tex! Come here. Right over here. Don't trip on that wreckage."

Firing the last shots allowed by the exhausted phaser banks, Dax glanced over her shoulder and saw a lanky stranger picking his way toward them. Longish brown hair, dirty, humanoid.

"From the planet?" she asked.

"Couldn't have done it without him. You should see these weapons he's got!"

"Chief," Dax said quietly, "the Prime Directive . . ."

O'Brien cocked his hip, winced, and drawled, "Not a problem. Lost Earth colony. I'll explain later."

As the ship streaked away from the planet, still pursued, still in trouble, Dax reached to clasp Tex's hand. "Welcome to Starfleet. Doctor, show this man to a post in the security team."

Bashir beamed with relief and even delight. "Yes, Captain!"

CHAPTER
9

"THERE WERE *several casualties, Captain. General Martok lost his second officer and two senior engineers. Eight of our lower-deck crew were killed in the ship's outer areas. Thank you for asking about Alexander.*"

"How many Jem'Hadar ships did you manage to draw away, Worf?"

Sisko leaned forward and peered at the communications screen, at Worf's dogged face with its constant scowl.

On the screen, the cross between the Empire and Starfleet looked as drawn as Sisko had seen him in weeks.

"*We engaged at least five Jem'Hadar,*" Worf told

him, *"but we have no way of knowing how many guard ships were left for Dax to face in the cluster."*

Sisko started to mention that they didn't even know yet whether or not the *Defiant* had survived the dangerous travel through the erupting core of the cluster to engage any Jem'Hadar ships that might be left behind. He would've voiced his concern, except that the captain of that ship was engaged to the man he was speaking to and Sisko was sensitive to reminding Worf that his fiancée might now be dead.

Besides, they both knew all the hard truths as well as their own names. There was no comfort either would take, or would attempt to give.

Worf waited through their mutual discomfort, then found a nonemotional question to ask. *"Has there been any news, sir?"*

Sisko almost winced. It was emotional anyway. "None."

"The Defiant *has been gone over sixteen hours."*

Finally Sisko had to offer something, anything. "I know this is difficult for you, Worf."

"Yes, sir," Worf accepted, *"but I sense it is more difficult for you. The* Defiant *is your ship."*

Of course, he wasn't just talking about the ship, Sisko knew. Worf was offering some kind of sympathy for Sisko's having to stay here, in this office, unable to share the pains or problems of his crew, and a simple order or change of position couldn't stop those people out there from being his crew.

"Dax'll bring her home," he said, mustering a hint of confidence. "There's no way she's going to miss her own wedding."

"No," Worf said. *"I suppose not."*

For a moment longer they regarded each other, neither willing to forfeit the stronger position in a relationship that now, though rarely, needed somebody to be the comforting one.

"As soon as I hear something," Sisko offered, "I'll let you know."

"Thank you, sir. Captain, you should get some rest."

Sisko almost straightened in the chair, but trying to pretend he wasn't exhausted would look just as silly as pretending he wasn't worried.

"Not tonight."

Without further amenities, Worf simply clicked off the communication. Neither of them wanted to hear any good-byes or over-and-outs.

"I've got to get out of here somehow," he murmured. "I've got to get back in command . . ."

Only the whispering hum of the hardworking tactical computer and the bubble of the replicator making him another cup of coffee provided any answer for his horrible mumble.

Get out. Get back command. Big talk from a selfish man. How many other Starfleet officers were hungering right now, as he was, for command? To get back their chance, their dignity, their grip on the twisting and turning of this war?

Strange—so often the image of people in a war was one of disgust, turning their backs, resisting the terrible occurrences, wishing to blind themselves from the sights and deafen the noises, but that wasn't the reality. War, yes—a thousand ugly images, but the great halo was enthusiasm and devotion, the fire with which so many quiet people stood up and asked to fight. There were many, many individuals out there right now who wanted a chance to strike, as did Ben Sisko. Why should he, instead of anyone else, get that chance? Unlike many, he hadn't lost crewmates or a ship yet. He had only lost a command. Even the station was not gone, not destroyed. It was still out there, intact, functioning somehow under the tricky pact he had forged between the Dominion and Bajor in order to keep the planet and station from being decimated.

He'd had an evacuation. Some embarrassment. Other than that, why was he feeling sorry for himself?

Ah—this jumble of mental blades! War could strip down a man's sense of solidity. He didn't know anymore what he used to know for sure. Where he belonged, who was his to worry about, where his son was, and the focus of his existence. Now everything was out of focus. Worf with Martok, Dax and the ship and crew off on a deadly mission without him, the station shrouded in silence, Jake unaccounted for, and Ben Sisko himself here giving advice to an admiral about tactical situations he had no experience with, in places he'd never even passed through.

He wanted focus. He wanted a victory, so he could shrug off this promotion.

How often could an officer say that?

Whatever happened, from now on he would be searching for a plan, a route, a plot, a chance to make a great stride and somehow keep Admiral Ross from making him a permanent fixture here at the nest, while eagles soared elsewhere.

"What the hell happened? Why didn't you disable the alarm!"

Kira Nerys was barely inside Odo's quarters when the question bolted from her lips.

He was here—in a cloudy sense of the word—regarding her with a glazed expression, a cold Founder-like serenity.

Would he have a reason for this? Could a shapeshifter get drunk? Hypnotized?

She didn't even have to ask what stopped him from tripping the alarm. She already knew that. The female shapeshifter had been in here again and they'd done that melting thing. The mystery was what had happened to Odo's sense of responsibility and loyalty to people who were risking their lives and depending on him to do his part in a plan he agreed with.

"It's difficult to explain," he murmured.

"Rom is sitting in a holding cell, being interrogated!" she charged without waiting for any explanation.

"I know . . ."

"You know? Do you realize you handed the Alpha Quadrant to the Dominion?"

"I was in the link . . ."

"Are you telling me you *forgot?*"

Seeming to glaze more deeply with every passing second, Odo blinked slowly. "I didn't forget . . . it just . . . didn't seem to matter . . ."

"A lot of people are going to die! Don't you care?"

Never in a decade would Kira have expected the answer that burbled from her old friend in the next seconds. He paused, searched for a way to say what he was thinking, or dreaming.

"It has nothing to do with me."

Stunned and willing to show it, Kira gaped at him. Was it really Odo sitting here or was this some kind of cruel game by the female shapeshifter? Was this a Founder's idea of a joke?

Suddenly cold all over, she gasped, "How can you say that?"

"If you could experience the link," he attempted weakly, "you'd know why nothing else matters . . ."

The room turned colder, darker somehow. Kira felt as if her feet were anchored to the deck, her arms transforming to iron blocks. She waited, but he made no change, no punch line, no excuses.

Destroying the antigraviton beam and preventing the Dominion from pulling down the minefield was a simple gesture upon which the lives of uncounted billions of people rested, and Odo was casting off its importance as a general nothing. The fate of the Alpha Quadrant had been his to implement, and he had let it slough away like runoff after rain.

On top of that, he had also cast off all the personal investments they had made in each other, and their friends had made in them. And the captain and the station—everything.

"The last five years," she rasped, "your life here . . . our friendship . . . none of that matters?"

He hesitated. He seemed almost to be having trouble even remembering. "It did . . . once . . ."

Kira tried to come up with something to say. But what was left? Had everything she thought had bonded them to each other over these years now become simply a forgettable lie?

"I wish I could make you understand," Odo said sadly, almost pityingly. "But you can't . . . you're not a changeling."

So now they were on different sides. The line was drawn. With the full measure of what she believed was happening here, Kira took a defining step backward.

"That's right," she said. "I'm a 'solid.'"

As the dividing line between them dropped to the floor and took a set in the mud of disappointment, Kira gave one last second's pitiful hope a moment to dissolve, then turned and left him behind, where he chose to be.

"I'm going to die."

Strange how much Rom's voice can sound like mine when he's whining.

Quark shook away the realization of familiar suffering techniques and flinched uneasily as, beside him, Leeta fought back tears at the sight of Rom inside the holding cell. The soft buzz of the force-field was a constant reminder that there would be no reaching out, no hugs, no hopes for mercy, especially not from the Jem'Hadar guard standing right over there.

"Stop saying that," Leeta gasped at her precious other.

"I didn't say it," Rom snapped. *"He* did."

And he pointed at Quark.

Stung, Quark irritably countered, "What I said is that they're *planning* to execute you. It's not the same as an execution order. Not yet, anyway."

"It is to me."

"Rom," Leeta interrupted, "we're not going to let them hurt you. Kira has gone to the Bajoran Council of Ministers. She's asking them to lodge an official protest."

"That's sweet. But I doubt it'll do any good."

Quark waved a hand. "And I've talked to Grand Nagus Zek himself and he's offered to buy your freedom from the Dominion."

Rom's thin lips peeled back from his filed teeth. "I don't think Weyoun cares much for latinum. I'm a dead man."

Without a beat, Leeta broke into sobs.

Quark felt his expression twist. "Would you please stop upsetting Leeta?"

"Sorry." Rom shifted uneasily, but given the circumstances he was taking all this better than Quark had anticipated. He figured he'd have two sobbing lumps on his hands instead of just one.

"Besides," Quark went on, "you think your big brother is going to let anything happen to you?"

"What can you do?" Rom asked reasonably.

"I'm not sure. But I'll think of something. No matter what it takes. No matter what I have to do, I'm going to get you out of here."

Leeta turned soggy eyes of gratitude upon him. "Oh, Quark—you do that and I'll work your dabo tables for free!"

"For how long?"

"An entire year!"

"Make it two."

"Brother!" Rom barked, cutting off the bargain.

Oh, well, couldn't blame a Ferengi for trying. "Isn't your life worth three years?" Quark spat through the forcefield. "Now sit tight and trust your older brother."

"But I don't want you to try to save me."

What? Had he said that? Leeta seemed surprised too. What kind of talk was that?

Quark squinted. "What kind of talk is that?"

"What are you talking about!" Leeta demanded at the same time. "They must've done something to his mind!"

Quark smirked. "What mind?"

"I'm serious," Rom insisted. "Brother, you have more important things to worry about."

"The bar's doing fine," Quark assured. "But thanks for caring."

"I'm not talking about the bar."

"Rom," Leeta broke in, "what could be more important than your life?"

Instantly he said, "Destroying the antigraviton beam to prevent the Dominion from taking down the minefield." He looked at Quark and stepped as close to the forcefield as he could get without burning his considerable nose. "You've got to finish what I started! The fate of the entire Alpha Quadrant rests in your hands. Billions and billions of people are counting on you!"

Quark drifted back a step and clutched his head. "Boy, are *they* gonna be disappointed!"

"Brother, you can do this! You *have* to do this. You *will* do this!"

"What happens if I get caught!"

"Then we'll die together. Side by side, heads held high, knowing we did our best."

Caught up in his own vision of noble self-sacrifice, Rom gazed at the far wall as if watching a tape of his own heroism.

Leeta warmed to the forcefield until it started to crackle. "Oh, Rom . . ."

"But I don't want to die," Quark complained.

"If that's what's written," Rom girded up, "then that's what's written. Now get going, brother. You have a lot of work to do."

"Father, I need to talk to you."

As his daughter's voice lightened Dukat's office, he looked up and smiled, accepting her kiss on his cheek.

"Is something wrong, my dear?" he asked.

"Nothing that *you* can't fix."

His daughter was a joy indeed. If only he'd known earlier in her life what it meant to have a decent young person to claim as his own—what others were missing who didn't anchor themselves in the future with children! If only he'd known.

"Name it," he offered.

Ziyal smiled, and Dukat was warmed by her reaction to his power, his control over the station, his status as imperial overlord of the quadrant. For this moment, all his power and influence meant nothing more to him than whatever it could do to make Ziyal smile again.

She virtually bounced before him. "I want you to free Rom."

His own smile dropped away. "You're joking . . ."

Ziyal's smile also dissolved, and she seemed surprised. "Not at all."

"I can't free Rom," Dukat told her. "He's been sentenced to death by the Dominion. Ziyal . . . this isn't a game or a piece of art. He committed an act of terrorism against the Dominion. He tried to inter- fere with our efforts to bring down the minefield. The self-replicating mines were his idea in the first place. He's not just Quark's sluggish brother any- more—he must be made an example so others don't make the same mistake."

"He's married to a Bajoran citizen," Ziyal at- tempted. "Doesn't that mean something?"

Dukat stood up. "As far as Weyoun is concerned, all that matters is that Rom's wife isn't also a conspirator or the Dominion would happily execute her too. Her Bajoran heritage buys only her life, not Rom's. Weyoun is completely unaffected by the formal protest from the Bajoran Council of Minis- ters. The planet simply doesn't mean as much to them as you might hope. Things will not likely go well for Bajor when the minefield comes down and the Dominion fleet comes through—"

"You can pardon Rom," Ziyal encouraged, a lilt of hope in her voice. "Don't you see, Father? This is your chance to show the Bajoran people—to show Major Kira—who you *really* are! A forgiving, com- passionate man . . . a great man!"

In the midst of her enthusiasm for his reputation, Dukat sensed something else and it worried him. He took her hands in his and fixed his gaze upon her.

"Tell me, Ziyal . . . were you involved in any way with the plan to sabotage the station?"

She yanked her hands away. "No, I wasn't involved!"

"You're sure of that? I can't help you unless you tell me the truth."

"I *am* telling you the truth!" she insisted. "The question is, have you been telling *me* the truth!"

Dukat tipped his head. "About what?"

"That the Bajorans are wrong about you! That you regret the horrible things you had to do during the occupation."

"I do regret them," he told her. "Deeply."

"Then this is your chance to prove it to everyone, including me!" Her eyes lit with possibility. "Show us that you're capable of mercy!"

But even for his daughter, Dukat knew he couldn't forfeit the control upon which the future turned so tenuously.

He shook his head. "Rom is an enemy of the state. And enemies of the state don't deserve mercy."

Ziyal grew cold before him. "Spoken like a true Cardassian."

"I am a Cardassian. And so are you."

"No." She pressed back, avoiding his attempt to take her hands again. "I'm not. I could never be like you."

She turned with a brief scorching glare, and when she had gone he felt burned.

The pressure from many quarters had been growing lately. He didn't like it. Cardassians pressuring him to subordinate the Jem'Hadar soldiers to them, Jem'Hadar Firsts insisting they should be treated like superiors because they were the fighting arm of the Dominion, Weyoun pressuring him to bring down the minefield, and all the time Dukat pressuring himself to stall that process while he built authority here and gave Cardassia a chance to rebuild.

Now these pressures were beginning to crack his shields. He couldn't give Ziyal what she wanted just because she wanted it. Yes, she was half Bajoran, struggling to be accepted on the planet, but large stakes to her became small when placed upon the desk of Gul Dukat.

Weyoun—the Vorta was a problem much harder to ignore. Pressure to bring down the minefield had finally become inexorable, and this coincided, luckily or unluckily, with Damar's idea to use the station's deflectors as an antigraviton weapon against the mines. Well, nothing lasted forever. Cardassia had been given a breathing spell, Dukat was firmly ensconced in authority here, and the Jem'Hadar were no longer sure whether they or the Cardassians were the supreme military force here. There might be a period of unbalance when the Dominion's first surge of reinforcements came through the wormhole, but Dukat believed he could hold out and continue the processes that he had been able to put into play over the past months.

He would have no choice. The minefield was coming down. Slowly, but it would come down now.

"Damar to Dukat."

"Dukat here."

"We're about to start firing the antigraviton beam, sir."

"Inform Weyoun. He won't want to miss it, I imagine."

"Must I?"

"Yes, Damar, you must. Don't worry, I'll make sure you get credit for the antigraviton idea."

"Should I tell Weyoun to come to your office?"

"We wouldn't be able to see the wormhole from here. Besides, I don't like having him in my office. Tell him to meet me in the wardroom."

"Yes, sir."

A relatively short trip a quarter of the way around the station's ring, roughly between his office and Ops, was the officers' wardroom, with its large viewport overlooking the area where the wormhole existed, now shrouded in its dark repose. When the minefield came down, the surge of Dominion ships from inside would trigger the vortex. The great swirling maw would open and offer them entry to the Alpha Quadrant.

Couldn't be put off forever, apparently.

Still haunted by his encounter with Ziyal, his daughter's disappointment in him churning in his gut, Dukat entered the wardroom to find that Weyoun was already there.

"Ah . . . just in time for the show," Dukat offered. "I have succeeded, as I assured you I would, in conquering the ingenious minefield."

"After so many months," the Vorta's milky voice returned, "I'm glad you finally succeeded. It has been pitiful to have such a meager thing as a string of mines preventing the Dominion from opening the wormhole."

"Meager?" Dukat huffed. "Hardly."

"As long as it is coming down."

"As I said it would. Damar is about to begin. If you'll join me at the viewport—"

Weyoun moved to the port, standing no nearer than absolutely necessary to Dukat, and together they watched the black curtain of space in which there seemed to be nothing, but in which there was actually much.

They stood for several seconds, waiting, not speaking.

Just when the pressure of silence began to mount, a tiny flash erupted in the distant blackness.

"There!" Dukat pointed out the port.

"Where?"

"Over there. That flash of light was the antigraviton beam hitting a mine."

"And disabling its replication unit?"

"Exactly. Didn't you see it?"

"I'm afraid not."

Exasperated, Dukat sighed. "For months you've been demanding that I take down those mines and now that it's finally happening, you can't even see it?"

"Weak eyes."

Weyoun turned and walked away from the port.

Dukat turned. "Excuse me?"

"My people have poor eyesight," the Vorta claimed. "It's something we've learned to live with. The Jem'Hadar, on the other hand, have excellent vision. I suppose they need it more than we do. I suppose I'll have to take your word for it."

Not about to fall for this, Dukat was determined to master the moment. "Once we've disabled the replication units in all the mines, we can detonate the entire minefield. And I guarantee, weak eyes or not, *that* explosion you will see."

Weyoun faced him. "When will you be ready to proceed?"

"Approximately seventy-eight hours. Three more days, and we can start bringing Jem'Hadar reinforcements through the wormhole."

And that victory will be mine, due to the efforts of Cardassians, not yours or any Vorta's.

Too excited to contain himself or pretend he didn't adore the idea of the falling minefield, Weyoun drew a sustaining breath. "Excellent. I knew you could do it, Dukat."

Dukat pressed his lips flat. "Did you?"

"I never doubted you for a moment."

Before Dukat could respond, the door opened and

Damar strode in, fresh off his victory of killing the first mine. Though his pride showed in his face, he controlled the moment by not mentioning the mine-field.

"Sir, I have new information on enemy fleet movements."

"Go ahead," Dukat responded.

"The allied Second Fleet has fallen back past the Kotanka System, while the Fifth Fleet has pulled out of the fighting along the Vulcan border." He crossed to a wall monitor and tapped a few keys, until a star chart came up. "Both fleets have converged here, at Starbase 375."

The ghostly face flashed in Dukat's mind. "Isn't that where Captain Sisko is stationed?"

Damar nodded. "He's been made an adjutant to Admiral Ross."

"Good for him," Weyoun clipped. "Now, why have those fleets gathered there?"

"I'm not sure."

"You're not sure? Two large enemy fleets break off from the front lines to rendezvous at a starbase and you have no idea why?"

Moving between them, Dukat said, "We'll have to find out, won't we?"

Weyoun nodded. "See that you do."

In a state of reined worry, he quickly left the room. Damar watched the Vorta leave and waited until the door swished closed.

"He should speak to you with greater respect."

"One day," Dukat said, "I'll let you teach him that lesson. But right now, there's something more pressing I need you to do. It's of a personal nature . . . a matter of some delicacy. It's about my daughter."

Damar seemed confused at being brought into the familiar circle. "Ziyal?" he asked, as if Dukat had any other daughter on DS9.

"We've had a misunderstanding," Dukat explained. "I want you to go and convince her to speak with me."

"Sir . . . I really think I could be more valuable tracking that enemy fleet—"

"I've given you an order, Damar. We're on the verge of a great victory. When it comes, I want my daughter at my side. Is that understood?"

No, it wasn't, Dukat knew, but what Damar understood didn't matter. He couldn't go himself, and he couldn't send anyone else. If Damar approached Ziyal, she would know for certain that her father was sincere enough to send his busy aide, interrupt station business and the trouble of an interstellar war just to tell her that she was important to him. It was a good signal. Damar would go. He might stall for a few days, but eventually, he would do as Dukat ordered. Dukat hoped he could predict what Ziyal would think about the gesture.

What Damar thought about it . . . Dukat cared not at all.

* * *

"Nausicaans? You can't trust them."

"I trust latinum. And so do they."

Quark poured a warm cup of raktajino for Major Kira and put it on the bar before her.

"Five bars will buy me five Nausicaans, a fast ship, and very few questions. Breaking Rom out of the holding cell will be child's play compared to the things they're used to doing."

"Forget it, Quark," she drawled. "Freeing Rom is going to take careful, precise planning. That's not the Nausicaan way. They're thugs. They'll come strutting onto the station, look at the Jem'Hadar the wrong way, and the next thing you know there'll be blood on the Promenade."

Quark shrugged. As if that would be a bad thing . . . then again, if she was right, there might be a security crackdown and Rom would be in even worse trouble. Although worse than a death sentence was hard to envision.

"Think I can get my money back?" he asked.

Before she could answer, they were both graced with the presence of Damar pressing up to the bar. "Major," the Cardassian said, "a freighter loaded with Tammeron grain is due to arrive within the hour. See to it that Cargo Bay Five is ready to receive it."

Kira looked at him as if wondering why he felt the need to tell her about a freighter that was still an hour away. "I'll take care of it," she said.

"Yes, you will. Now."

She glared at him, irritated. Quark watched the two of them, the interplay of venom coursing along between them, and enjoyed his part in it. Damar was here because Quark now had tacit control over him, and nobody knew it. Damar wanted Kira to leave so he could be alone with his wondrous guru—the provider of the ancient kanar laced with . . . trade secrets.

"That attitude of yours, Major," Damar warned, "it won't be tolerated forever."

Pushing off her stool, Kira responded, "You don't like my attitude, Damar? You're welcome to try and change it."

Quark reached for the special decanter of kanar. Damar watched Kira leave, then said, "I don't understand what Dukat sees in that woman."

"Then you need to get your eyes examined. One kanar. Want me to leave the bottle?"

Damar nodded. He eyed the decanter. "Maybe I should have you taste it first. Make sure it isn't poisoned."

Quark smiled. "Poisoning customers is bad for business."

"True," Damar accepted, "but some people might place a brother's revenge above business."

"Not this Ferengi," Quark told him. He was supremely confident. Damar would trust him implicitly after the first sip, when the drugged kanar triggered reactivation of the previous session.

This had been going on for weeks now. Damar had no idea he was drawn to the bar by any but his own inner controls. He also had no idea that his inclination to trust Quark was anything less than his own solid judgment.

After the first swig, predictably, Damar was almost immediately gazing at him with unshielded respect. "You're a credit to your race, Quark," the aide said. "Unlike your brother, you've chosen to back the winning side."

"Mmm." Quark poured him another drink—all the way up to the rim this time. "All right . . . are you going to tell me, or do you want me to guess?"

Damar's eyes were already glazing. "Tell you what?"

"Don't be coy with me. Either someone you don't like has died or your promotion came through."

"It's better than that." Damar took a long drag on the kanar, swallowed laboriously, then steadied himself. "It's about the minefield."

"What about it?"

The Cardassian leaned closer and lowered his voice. "It's coming down."

Unimpressed, Quark fished for more information with, "I've heard that before."

Damar took another sip. "Remember those field tests I was telling you about? They were successful. We've begun to deactivate the mines."

Forcing his expression to feign something other

than the worry he felt, Quark nodded. "Well . . . you've got your work cut out for you. What's it going to take? A couple of months? A year?"

Damar smiled ridiculously. "One week."

"A *week?*" Quark gulped. "One week to take down hundreds upon hundreds of mines in a grid half the size of a planet?"

Leaning back and pressing his wrists in satisfaction to the bar, Damar cupped a hand around his glass.

"That's right," he said. "One week . . . and the Alpha Quadrant will be ours!"

CHAPTER
10

"A WEEK? You're sure about that?"

Kira blurted her questions so loudly that she had to draw back quickly and hope nobody heard over the noise of the bar's customers and the dabo tables.

"That's what he said," Quark told her, "and believe me, it was no idle boast."

"We've got to stop them . . ."

"And end up sharing a cell with my brother? No, thanks. If we could only get to Odo . . . make him see what's going on. He'd have to help us—"

"Forget about Odo," Kira ordered in an unkind way, peeved at being reminded that she hadn't been able to see Odo and that he'd been holed up in his quarters with that excuse for a female, enjoying the "link" while the Alpha Quadrant shuddered around them. "First, we can't get to him. And second, he wouldn't help us if we did."

Quark filled a warm glass for her, even though she hadn't ordered anything. They had to keep up appearances. "Then what we have to do," he said, "is warn Starfleet."

She looked up. "And how do you suggest we get a message out to them?"

"You're asking me? You're the terrorist. I'm just a bartender."

Kira appreciated his attempt at a joke, but it didn't make her feel any better. A week . . . if the minefield went down that soon, if Starfleet were taken by surprise by a huge fleet of Dominion ships, Bajor and the station would be overwhelmed, the war could be over in a matter of days, and the Dominion would rule the quadrant.

Pausing in the middle of chaos to stretch a muscle in her back, she groaned inwardly as Jake Sisko sauntered to them with that postpubescent grin. That's all she needed—

"From the look on your faces," the young man said, "I can see you haven't had much luck getting Rom out of jail."

"And the news just keeps getting worse," Quark finished.

Jake settled onto a stool. "It's not all that bad."

"Trust us, Jake," Kira grumbled, "it is."

"Not for me. I'm getting a message through to my dad."

Kira straightened instantly. "How?"

"I'm a reporter. I have my ways."

"Jake! This is no time for games!"

Smiling, he turned and pointed at a nearby table, where one of the bar's regulars, a sluglike creature they all knew well, was using his huge mitts to fumble a ribbon around a box. He almost never spoke, and he sure couldn't tie a bow.

"Morn?" Kira asked.

"He's going home for his mother's birthday or something. He has an encrypted message for my dad in one of her presents."

"Of course!" Kira knotted her shoulders with anticipation. "I cleared him over to Cardassian customs with a limited visa myself! Do you think this can work?"

Jake leaned toward her. "It's already working. The Cardassians know him and don't think he's smart enough to be involved in any kind of espionage. They're taking bets about whether he'll even be able to find his way to his mother's colony!"

"Bets?" Quark perked up. "Who's brokering the bets?"

"Down, Quark," Kira said. "This isn't the time for you to be skimming. Let's just very quietly go over there . . . and have a drink with our old pal Morn."

* * *

So far, so good. Morn didn't even want to know what information he was carrying. Kira checked him onto the cargo freighter herself, knowing that he would quietly move across the lines, then funnel the news about the minefield's imminent fall through to Captain Sisko. Almost time to launch . . .

Clear them through the station's security codes . . . good. One more level . . . release the docking clamps . . . cleared for launch.

Good-bye, Morn. Work fast. Only days to go.

How long would it take him to get the message through to Captain Sisko? They only had a week, and Starfleet would need time to pull together an offensive that suddenly. Kira's head swam as she tried to avoid imagining that kind of hustling.

"Nerys?"

She flinched, and wheeled around—"Ziyal?"

A movement in the shaded outlines of the docking-ring cargo bay drew her eye, and Dukat's daughter stepped toward her, almost shy in her manner.

Kira let out a relieved huff. "Ziyal."

"Can I talk to you?" the girl said. "I need to talk to *somebody* . . . and it's been so long since we've spent any time together—"

"I told you," Kira said, finishing the closeouts on the launch sequence, "you shouldn't have to choose between me and your father. I don't expect that. He's your father."

Ziyal pressed her shoulder against the nearest

bulkhead and gazed at the carpet. "I thought things would be better. I thought we could move toward some kind of peace between Bajor and Cardassia."

"You can't hope for that, Ziyal, just because you're half of each. Real life doesn't work that way. Your blood isn't really half one and half the other— and you are who you want to be, not a divided person. Bajor and Cardassia have different visions of what life should be. They can't just sit back and smile at each other. And they shouldn't have to."

Ziyal nodded sadly. "I really believed that my father had changed . . . that he wanted to be a man of peace."

"I think he believes that, too, whenever it suits his purpose."

"Everything he's ever said to me has been a lie."

Kira looked at her. Couldn't let things go that far, could she? "Not everything. He really does care for you."

"I don't care," the girl protested. "I'm not going back to him. You don't believe that, do you?"

Letting the transfer sequence and the refueling log take care of itself, Kira turned away from the panel. "Right now, you're angry and disappointed. But that'll pass. And then you'll have to decide what to do."

Ziyal started to say something else, but the nearest doors parted. Damar.

"Ziyal," the Cardassian blurted immediately, "I need to speak to you."

"You and I have nothing to talk about," she told him.

He squared off before them. "Maybe not. But you and your father do. He wants to see you."

"Well, I don't want to see him."

Kira motioned toward the doors. "You heard her, Damar."

"Stay out of this, Major. Listen to me, Ziyal. Your father is a great man. A man of destiny. But he also carries great burdens. He knows our alliance with the Dominion is a dangerous one. If we show any sign of weakness, our allies will turn on us. That's why we must all help your father remain strong. So I ask you to be a true daughter of Cardassia and stand beside him."

"It should be obvious," Ziyal said, "even to you, Damar, that I am not a 'true daughter of Cardassia.'"

"What's obvious to me," he said through gritting teeth, "is that your father should've left you to rot in that Breen prison camp. But he didn't. He took pity on you and it's your duty to repay him. Now, come with me."

He grasped her arm and physically turned her toward the doors.

Enough. Kira reached out and pushed him. "Leave her alone."

Delighting in the situation, Damar snarled, "And if I don't?"

"I was hoping you'd ask."

Kira knew she was a narrow sort of person with tiny hands and not much muscle, but she was also a trained resistance fighter who had never forgotten a few key weaknesses in Cardassian physiology. Damar, on the other hand, was a drowsy bureaucrat who hadn't physically fought with anybody in years. He also never expected her to actually hit him. Add to that concoction about three months of frustration to work off, and Kira had plenty of crushing force to deliver.

Jaw, gullet, secondary rib cage—bony brow. Down he went.

Now she had a sore hand, a bruised set of knuckles, and a deep breath of satisfaction. That felt *great!*

Ziyal stepped back, her arms flared, and gaped at the lump of Damar on the deck. "Did you kill him?"

"No, but I thought about it."

"What are you going to do when he wakes up?"

"That's up to him. Let's get out of here."

"Ben? Ben! You in here?"

"I'm in the anteroom, Admiral—what's wrong?"

"The *Defiant's* just docking up! I wanted to tell you myself instead of over the comm. I wanted to see your face."

"Well, here it is!" Ben Sisko finished changing into a fresh uniform and bolted out of the anteroom into the main area of his office, to find Admiral Ross standing there like a kid about to go to a season-ender. "Why didn't they call in?"

"Their whole comm system's down. I didn't even know they were on approach until the lightship notified my liaison at the dockmaster's office."

Sisko rushed out into the corridor and headed for the nearest turbolift, with Admiral Ross jogging after him. He dodged into the lift and barely waited for Ross to get in before ordering, "Internal space-dock, slip number 11."

"No, Ben," Ross corrected. "They'll be debarking to the mess hall. The ship had to be cleared immediately. Toxic leaks."

"Leaks?" Sisko frowned. "Damn that cluster . . ."

Ross didn't respond. There was nothing much to say—they had no information about how many casualties—

"Wait a minute," Sisko blurted suddenly. "If they're on the station—" He tapped his combadge. "Sisko to Dax. Are you reading?"

Dax here. We're docked and debarked. O'Brien's overseeing the preliminary diagnostics. Mission accomplished—the array is down.

A light-headed relief almost lifted him off his feet. "Congratulations, old man, and good work. What are your losses?"

Six dead, fifteen injuries, two serious. Julian's already released several of them, and the two criticals have been moved to the Starbase infirmary under care of the new trauma team. I relieved Julian of responsibility for them and ordered him to stand down. He was about to stay up another thirty-six hours and try to care for them himself. Instead, he's down here with me, flirting with a pretty ensign."

"We're almost there, Dax."

Ross smiled. "Tell them we're recommending them for E.P.D. citation."

Sisko returned the smile. "Dax, the admiral is recommending you and the whole crew for exceptional performance of duty citations."

"That's very gracious, and I think we'll just take those and retire to a sunny climate."

"We don't blame you."

"See you in a minute. Dax out."

"They sure sound proud of themselves," Ross said. "I can't wait to read their report. Bet it beats its way to the top of the best-seller list."

"I'll bet it will." Swimming in relief and satisfaction, Sisko couldn't stop smiling. Why was this turbolift going so slowly? "Sir, if you're in agreement, I'd also like to recommend that Cadet Nog be given a promotion to ensign."

"How close is he to graduating from the Academy?"

"Close enough to risk his life on a virtually suicidal mission through the Argolis Cluster."

"Good point. Recommendation accepted. Now you tell me . . . how can you grin like that? There are six dead people over there. Some of them might be your closest friends."

"It's a chance we take," Sisko told him, for a moment enjoying the superiority of having commanded a small ship, when he knew Ross never had a command that intimate, and never during a major conflict. "If we'd lost any of our immediate family, Dax would've sounded different. I'd have known. She mentioned O'Brien and Bashir, so they're all right, but . . . I know it seems callous. Losing any shipmate is hard, even if we don't know that person, but we all know why we're fighting and what the risks are. It's not as if anyone signed on for active duty without understanding. We all accept that, Admiral . . . and none of us want to be mourned too much. It's the last gift we can give each other."

Ross seemed momentarily circumspect. "I'll remember that. As soon as O'Brien's diagnostic is finished, we'll start repairs on the *Defiant* and get her restaffed."

Now, at a note he'd come to recognize in the admiral's tone, Sisko dropped his smile. "What's the rush, sir? They just came in."

"I know," Ross said, and sighed. "And they're going right back out. I'm taking your recommendation of immediate action in Bravo, Delta, and Zebra sectors. Now that the sensor array is down, we can make those major strikes we've been holding back on. We can move ships and squadrons, and we've got to do it before the Dominion gets any more advantages. Now, don't look at me like that. This is *your* plan. We don't have time for shore leaves or mollycoddling. I want you to make a plan for Dax to hit one of those critical depots."

Sisko had let the admiral speak, hoping that at the bottom of all those words might be lurking a re-installation of himself as commander of the *Defiant*. No such luck. He'd made himself too valuable as a tactician.

They strode in rather odd silence to the mess hall and immediately swept inside. As the panels parted, a gush of noise and cheer rushed out and embraced them, drawing them inside. Sisko did an automatic head count of how many of the crew were here and who they were, but said nothing about it.

"Admiral on deck!" Nog shouted from the table where he was handing out drinks.

The crew snapped to attention, but Ross immediately said, "Carry on."

And they did. This time there was nothing sub-dued about their celebration, even with the admiral and his adjutant in attendance.

"Nog!" Dax called as she strode toward them, "Saurian brandy for the brass!"

Brass . . .

Just as Dax reached them, a slightly besotted Julian Bashir, with a bruise on his left temple, headed her off. "Dax! Would you tell Ensign Kirby how I took over the conn when Lieutenant Haj was injured during the attack? She doesn't believe me."

"Frankly," Dax demurred, "I'm not sure it really happened myself."

She gave him a scolding look, and only now Bashir realized he was standing with his back to Sisko and the admiral. He turned, made a polite, "Sir . . . sir," and melted back into the crew.

"Congratulations, Captain," Ross said to Dax.

"Thank you, sir. If you'll excuse me, I need to talk to Julian."

Sisko thought it was odd that she ducked away from them like that. Perhaps she was embarrassed to be in command of a ship she knew he wanted, or perhaps she was afraid the admiral might make that command permanent here and now if she lingered. He didn't know. He wasn't really in a position to ask, either. That wouldn't've been decorous.

Disturbed that things had changed so much between himself and his closest friends, Sisko accepted his brandy from Nog with less than rousing enthusiasm. He muttered something to Ross, but didn't even listen to himself.

He roused only when Miles O'Brien appeared, carrying another empty phaser canister. Sisko straightened his shoulders, towering over most of the crewmen here, but O'Brien didn't see him. Instead, he headed directly for Dax.

"Another one, Captain," the engineer said, and shifted the metal canister into Dax's arms.

Carrying it like a big ugly baby, Dax held the canister for all to see. "Take a good look! This says something about us. It says we're willing to fight and that we'll keep on fighting until we can't fight anymore."

"Yes, sir!" the crew predictably cheered.

"You don't throw something like this away!"

"No, sir!"

Just as Sisko had all the times before, Dax moved to the side of the mess hall and clanked the canister into place with all the others.

Sisko almost shriveled with embarrassment. Dax had used his exact words. He knew why—she was making an effort at tribute to him. But he didn't feel flattered by her effort. He felt shunted aside, pathetic, patronized.

"They're a good crew," Ross said quietly.

Cold and envious, worried about the new mission he would have to foist upon these people within a day, Sisko buried a shudder. "The best."

Ross was watching him. Knew. Saw.

"What do you say," the admiral wisely suggested, "we get back to work?"

Sisko hated him for understanding.

But followed Ross out. What else could he do?

Boldly they rode and well . . .

CHAPTER 11

"CADET?"

"Continuing to emit distress signals on all frequencies."

"Chief?"

"We're still venting plasma . . . any ship passing within a hundred million kilometers will know we're here . . . and that we're not going anywhere."

Miles O'Brien made his report tersely. They were adrift, leaking all the juices of life, engines cold.

This was how it had been for weeks. When the Dominion's sensor array fell, a flurry of confused offensive activity erupted among the Jem'Hadar forces. Afraid they'd be attacked all over the front, they took the offensive and began attacking anything they could find, any outpost, any ship, any squadron, any transport. Instead of picking and choosing, they were now trying to attack and defend everything. Yes, this was wearing the unreinforced, white-starved Dominion forces thin, but it was also taking tremendous effort on the parts of Starfleet and the Klingons just to keep up the level of harassment. There could be little forward movement—in fact, they'd almost reached a stalemate as far as progress was concerned. For a tie game, there were plenty of losses.

"In other words, we're sitting ducks," Julian Bashir wearily tacked onto O'Brien's tepid report.

"Looks that way," O'Brien confirmed.

Dax made no response to them, though O'Brien automatically glanced at her. They were all tense, focused, watching for the slightest miscalculation, each battling to keep from becoming casual about the danger or even about dying.

"We have company, Captain," Nog abruptly reported. "Two Dominion ships heading this way, bearing one-nine-seven mark one-three-five."

Just what they'd expected. O'Brien came to life instantly, then pulled his hands back from the automatic movements his fingers wanted to make. "They'll have us in weapons' range in twenty-two seconds."

Dax looked intently at the forward screen as two Jem'Hadar fighters streaked toward them. "Shields?"

Nog said, "Shields at thirty percent."

O'Brien planted both feet on the deck and prepared for what was coming.

"Phaser banks?" Dax asked.

"The entire weapons array is off line."

"What do we do now, Captain?" Bashir wondered.

Dax gripped her command chair as the first of the Jem'Hadar ships wheeled into weapons range. "Now we find something to hold on to."

Over the last of her words, they were strafed mercilessly. The shell of *Defiant* thundered around them, hammering their ears and their bodies with shock after shock. O'Brien had braced his legs on the deck, and now the deck surged, ramming his knees into the underdeck of his engineering panel.

"Shields are down to twenty percent," Nog reported.

O'Brien winced at his knees and the report. "I don't know how much more of this we can take—"

"Steady, people," Dax reminded.

The waiting was the worst. If this went on much longer—

"Look!" Nog shouted as the screen changed.

Now they could see a Klingon bird of prey, and how pretty it was, decloak behind one of the Dominion ships and blast it to shards.

"Now?" O'Brien asked.

"Now!" Dax sat up straighter. "Shields up, engines at full impulse, power to main phasers—"

"Target locked."

"Fire!"

Sitting ducks playing possum . . . they were every kind of animal but trapped. Around them, all systems surged to life with an audible hum, and the *Defiant* unloaded a barrage of phaser fire on the second Jem'Hadar ship. Before their eyes—and close enough to rattle their hull with shrapnel—the enemy ship was obliterated.

"Cadet," Dax instantly asked, "any more Dominion ships out there?"

"None that I can see."

Dax punched the shipwide comm. "This is the captain speaking. All hands, stand down. Good job, people."

"We're being hailed by the *Rotarran*," Nog said. "Commander Worf would like to speak to you."

"On screen."

The image of Worf—a welcome sight even though they'd been faking—gave O'Brien a rush of good cheer in the midst of the daily grind of stalemate, which was immediately crushed by an all-ships alert he picked up on officer-only comm reroute. As Dax greeted their "rescuers," O'Brien collected the communiqué.

"My hero." Dax was smiling.

"Well done, Captain," Worf responded. Not exactly a balcony scene. *"You were a very effective decoy."*

"How about next time we switch roles? That way, I can rescue you?"

O'Brien sighed. No getting around this. "You may have to wait awhile, Captain. We've just received orders from Starfleet Command. All ships in this sector are to fall back to Starbase 375."

She looked at him as if it were his fault. "Fall back again?"

The sense of victory now crumbled.

"Engage and retreat, engage and retreat," O'Brien chanted. "I'm telling you, that's become our favorite tune."

"Well," Bashir added, "we'd better learn a new one or the next song we'll be singing will be 'Hail the Conquering Dominion.'"

Irritated, Dax said, "I wouldn't start learning those lyrics just yet, Doctor. Worf, we'll see you at Starbase 375."

"I'll be waiting."

"Set a course for these coordinates, warp seven."

O'Brien pushed out of his chair and worked his bruised knees over to the command deck. "Is this a plan or isn't it? We're doing some kind of profitless waltz and it's getting harder and harder to explain."

"I know," she said.

"We're holding our own for now, but every exercise costs us in weapons and fuel, if not manpower."

"I know, Chief."

"The hardier souls among us might hope this was all part of a bigger plan Starfleet Command has for a few eventual forward movements, but from this level, it's a bit hard to see into the future."

"I know, I know."

"Captain Sisko must know what's going on . . . he keeps sending us out on these hit-and-runs. Maybe you could ask . . . I mean he *is* our . . ."

Failing a polite articulation, he gave up. His hand was making some pathetic waves, and now he turned it upward to give his head a scratch.

"If there isn't some kind of plan," Dax interrupted, "if this is just a holding pattern and all we're doing is keeping the Dominion from overrunning us, then eventually that minefield will fall and the enemy will get reinforcements. And we don't have any reinforcements to get. Fuel, weapons, manpower . . . the most dangerous loss is going to be the will to fight among the troops. And that's when we'll lose the war."

O'Brien leaned an elbow on the command chair to spare his throbbing knees, and felt the cloying pressure of reality depress his chest.

"I know," he said.

"Admiral, the time has come. There's only so much icy composure we can ask of our troops while we thin out the Dominion forces. We've brought the Dominion down to our level of military capability, but we haven't brought our own up any. We've weakened the enemy as much as we can, in my opinion, and the situation's getting precarious. It'll start tipping in the Dominion's favor again if we don't push it our way soon."

"I know."

Admiral Ross's response was not enheartening. Ben Sisko knew Ross had come to his office instead of the other way around in order to give him a little boost, and now he was talking to the admiral about giving everybody a boost. Wars could be won or lost on morale, and this one was on its firing line.

"You asked to see me," Ross went on, "so I'm going to assume you've got some big idea that you've had in mind while you implemented all these little ideas. Go ahead, Ben, you don't have to run around the perimeter with me."

The keen assessment of what Sisko had been doing was embarrassing in its accuracy, but Sisko couldn't resist a smile. He'd been in command in a distant post so long that he'd gotten used to being the smartest kid in class and knowing what was happening on many levels. Ross's bluntness disarmed him. How long had the admiral known Sisko was coyly magistrating an overriding plan?

Maybe this was why the admiralty held so few attractions for Sisko and many captains—because a good captain is a person able to find strength and abilities where there might appear to be few, to tease out and efficiently use the talents of whatever crew was assigned to him, without the ability to pick and choose people. An admiral had to be something else, and not everybody could do that.

Ross was like a very successful coach of a sports team. He couldn't hit a ball out of the park or race around the bases in a matter of seconds, but he had always had the ability to see who could and push them to do it. This made him very valuable to Starfleet. As an admiral, he might have twenty people telling him what to do. He was good at the important part—picking the right twenty people. Then, he was also good at deciding who was the most right of a lot of possible rights, and which of those was best to carry out those plans—not always the same people at all.

He was also smart enough to damned well realize he'd never commanded anything small and intimate. He couldn't count on his own experience for that kind of thing, and he was bright enough not to try.

As Sisko responded to a simple at-ease motion by Ross and settled back into his chair, he felt a flicker of respect for this man from whom he'd tried to keep his real intentions hidden. Ross did him a favor by sitting down also.

"We tied the score with the attack on the ketracel-white processing station," Sisko began. "Then we tipped it our way when we destroyed the sensor array. That gave us an opportunity to move our fleets and squadrons without the Dominion's knowing what we were doing. We've made strategic hits since then, but we've been asking a lot of our troops simply by not explaining any long-term plan to them."

"We couldn't," Ross said. "It's been the same for

every admiral. We're barely speaking to each other, for fear of hidden shapeshifter spies. It's very hard to coordinate anything."

For an instant Sisko held his breath, wondering if Ross's intuition had tipped him off about plans between Sisko and Martok, or if the admiral had noticed how many of Sisko's small mission plans had been enacted by Martok and the *Defiant*. Of course he'd noticed. How could he not?

But Ross spared him the further revealing. "You've been planning something," he urged. "Time to tell me."

Sisko nodded, thereby acknowledging that Ross had him and the time had indeed come.

"I want to make a comprehensive assault on the Bajoran system and repossess it before the minefield falls."

Ross blinked, then laughed openly. "You don't think small, do you? Do you know how *far* behind enemy lines Bajor is now? Never mind—of course you do. What do you think we'll need for this? No, don't tell me. Tell me *who* you'll need."

"Who . . . I'll need Martok and Worf . . . I'll need the Klingon Defense Forces—"

"All right, I'll see that Chancellor Gowron is contacted directly. How about if Worf or Martok talks to Gowron?"

"That's a very sound suggestion, sir."

"I'm known for those."

"I don't know how Worf will feel about it—he's

DIANE CAREY

not on the smoothest of terms with Gowron right now. But being approached by other Klingons of high family status in both fleets is something he can't ignore, at least. I'll need to present my strategic plans to the admiralty as soon as possible."

"How about 0800 tomorrow?"

Sisko sat back in surprise. That easily?

"Well," Ross said, reading his expression, "I was going to present my own plan, but it was only a couple of distraction skirmishes and a ground assault on Centaurus Nine. If you can do this, that won't matter. Why don't you take my segment of time before Command tomorrow morning?"

Shaking his head in admiration, Sisko dropped the last measure of protocol and decorum that was expected between a captain and an admiral, and looked at Ross with unshielded camaraderie.

"If either of us was as good at tactics as we were at lying," he said, "this war would've been won a month ago."

Ross clapped his knees and stood up. "Yeah, but we can learn. See you at 0800."

Flattered that the admiral didn't ask for specifics—probably he already suspected what his frustrated adjutant had in mind—Sisko didn't bother to stand up in polite escort of the admiral's leaving the office. Didn't seem necessary, somehow. The formality had gone out, blessedly, of their relationship. At least in private. Tomorrow morning, there would be another kind of dutiful performance.

Almost as soon as the admiral had gone, the door to Sisko's office slid open again without chimes, leading him for a moment to believe that Ross was coming back in, but rather it was Dax who entered, not looking very content at all.

"Why did you call us back?" she demanded without greeting. "All Starfleet ships in the area banding up here? What are we all doing here, Benjamin? Providing a target?"

Sisko regarded her with tolerance. "I haven't seen you angry in . . . oh, let's see . . ."

"I don't know what all you brass hats in Starfleet Command are thinking, but take it from a simple field officer, we're not going to win this war by running away from the enemy."

This made him bristle and his grin dropped away. Her unfairness surprised him. She wasn't usually petty or shortsighted enough to scratch a dividing line between them when she knew he wasn't here by choice or that the "brass hats" were carrying the weight of the future under their brims and they felt it every moment. She knew that. She *knew* that.

Choosing to remain silent, he simply looked at Dax and let her get the rest out.

"Benjamin," she went on, "troop morale is at an all-time low. Even the Klingons are starting to wonder if we can defeat the Dominion. We need a victory! A big victory. And we need it soon!"

"I couldn't agree with you more," he uttered.

"Then do something about it!"

"I have."

Perhaps his tone embarrassed her, reminded her of something she should be remembering on her own, but she suddenly backed off as if he had drenched her in cold water.

"In fact," he was proud to be able to say, "I'm presenting a plan to Starfleet Command at 0800 tomorrow."

Her doll-perfect face creased. "What plan?"

He tapped a panel. A familiar graphic, the most beautiful sight in the galaxy to both of them now, appeared on the office's big screen.

Sisko turned to regard it as if he were visiting a museum and had just found the show's signature piece.

"We're going to take back *Deep Space Nine.*"

Out-worn heart, in a time out-worn,
Come clear of the nets of wrong and right;
Laugh, heart, again in the grey twilight,
Sigh, heart, again in the dew of the morn.

William Butler Yeats,
Into the Twilight

CHAPTER
12

NOW THAT HE'D convinced himself and blithely announced his intentions to Dax and elicited Martok's assistance, there was only one obstacle. Just a little thing. Just Starfleet Command.

The Admiralty had a command unit in this sector consisting of three admirals—Ross, Coburn, and Sitak. Coburn was a middle-aged rear admiral, Sitak a seemingly ageless Vulcan vice-admiral, and the three of them made a formidable jury before which Sisko found himself pacing six days later.

Six days—he'd hardly had time to gather intelligence information about enemy-force positions that was fresh enough to use in an assault plan, never mind pull together statistical information on Starfleet deployment. Still, he was glad he'd tried to move faster than usual.

"I hope you'll all forgive my brazenness, but in my opinion," he told them, "we're making a mistake trying to put a wide-range defense perimeter around Earth and primary Federation colonies and trade routes."

"Those routes are critical, Captain," Sitak said. "The main arteries between Earth and Vulcan, Vulcan and Alpha Centauri . . . they're our life's blood. In any war, the first goal is to strangle the enemy. We dare not let the Dominion cut off the routes of supplies and arms to our colonies and outposts."

"And an attack on Earth would be a deadly blow if they succeeded," Coburn agreed. "Are you suggesting we should stop defending them?"

"Not at all," Sisko said. "But, so far, all we're doing is defense. We can't defend our way to victory. And by doing nothing but responding all the time, we're letting the Dominion set the pattern of events. Yes, Admiral Sitak, you're right—they're predictable. They're waging a war right out of the manual at least for now. If we're clever enough, we can use that against them. I don't actually believe they intend to keep it up. If they're planning to attack Earth, they're making a huge strategic mistake. I don't think they'll make it."

"Why don't you explain what you've got in mind?" Ross encouraged.

Sisko drew a tense breath and held it a little too long. He directed their attention to the wall-monitor display, on which he had arranged a design for attack.

"By putting together a task force comprised of elements from the Second, Fifth, and Ninth Fleets, I believe that we can take back *Deep Space Nine* . . . the most important piece of real estate in the quadrant."

Sitak immediately said, "Your plan, Captain Sisko, is not without merit, however I remain skeptical. The Dominion will undoubtedly send a large fleet to stop you."

"Which will divert their forces and slow their advance into Federation territory."

Ross tossed in, "As well as leave their flank vulnerable."

Sisko nodded. "Giving us a chance to go on the offensive for a change."

"There's one thing that concerns me," Coburn broke in.

"What's that, Admiral?"

"Earth. You've left it a very tempting target."

Ross pointed at the schematic. "Earth would still be defended by the Third Fleet."

"But what if you're wrong and the Dominion doesn't commit its forces to protect *Deep Space Nine?* What if they launch a full-scale assault on Earth instead?"

A moment of pause interrupted them as they all ran through the various scenarios in their minds. Sisko was very nervous suddenly—what if they thought he was trying to do this just to get his station back? What if they imagined his pride was bruised and he just wanted to recapture the station for his own reputation, or for the edification of his own crew? It looked that way, he had to admit, and he'd think that about anyone else suggesting such a risk.

Then Coburn squinted at the displays with a discerning eye. "If we do what you're proposing, we'll never get reinforcements there in time."

Sisko bluntly said, "The Dominion won't attack Earth."

Might as well get it out and let them think whatever they were bound to think.

Sitak turned to him. "How can you be sure?"

"Because Earth isn't the key to the Alpha Quadrant. The wormhole is. And whoever controls *Deep Space Nine* controls the wormhole."

Prejudice or predilection, there was no denying the simple truth of that. He was the gatekeeper, yes, but there had to be a gate and the gate had to be controlled. These were admirals, not idiots. They knew he was right.

He understood their point too—the need to protect what needed protecting, but also possess what needed to be possessed, and DS9 had already been lost once at great cost. So far the wormhole was still closed and the enemy fleet was being held off, but that couldn't last. A swarm of Dominion ships coming through the wormhole wouldn't be stopped once they flooded the quadrant. The only hope was to control the mouth of the wormhole.

Yes, he was right, and he made himself cling to his rightness. If they saw that he was confident, they might go his way.

He should argue his point again. Repeat everything. Point at the screens. Pound a table.

But he didn't. That would've been unprofessional. He'd made his statement. They either believed he was an expert on the Federation deep space perimeter or they didn't. Dramatic insistence would get him nothing but disrespect.

Then came the most amazing occurrence—Admiral Coburn simply asked, "Who've you got for backup?"

Sisko smiled like a schoolboy who'd just gotten his homework back with a good grade.

"Have you ever heard of General Martok?" he asked.

"Gentlemen, this mission cannot succeed without the involvement of the Klingon Defense Forces."

Sisko led the way into his office and motioned for Martok and Worf to sit down. The meeting with Starfleet Command, just an hour ago, had gone well enough, but left him holding a lot of balls and juggling like mad. Martok and Worf had remained quiet during the meeting, representing the willingness of the Klingon Empire to participate in Starfleet schemes. Now came the hard part—making good on that symbolism.

"We agree, Captain," Worf told him, "but Chancellor Gowron does not."

"Then you have to change his mind."

One ball, effectively tossed into somebody else's hands. Worf didn't appear surprised or very much bothered by the idea of confronting Gowron in person, but Martok shifted uneasily. The general, Sisko sensed, was displeased at the political aspect, of being pulled into such machinations by the thready relationship between the Federation and the Empire. It was unappealing, Sisko had to agree.

Martok glowered for a moment. "The chancellor is reluctant to commit such a large fleet to a single engagement."

Worf nodded. "He feels it would leave the Empire vulnerable."

Sisko appreciated the reports, and even more the fact that neither of these Klingons agreed with what they were having to say. He could tell that without asking a thing.

"Starfleet Command had the same concerns about Earth," he told them. "But after careful consideration, they decided it was worth the risk. We have to take some kind of decisive action in the Bajor area before that minefield comes down. That means taking back *Deep Space Nine* and doing it now, while the Dominion forces are at their weakest."

"General," Worf said, turning to Martok, "perhaps you should return to Qo'noS and make your plea in person. The chancellor has great respect for you. If you cannot persuade him, no one can."

"I will go see Gowron," Martok agreed, "and you will come with me."

Worf hesitated. "The chancellor no longer considers me a friend."

"I know. But what could be better—an ally and an enemy, both telling him the same thing. He'll have no choice but to agree."

Sisko regarded the general with a certain forbearance. No choice? There were plenty of choices. Martok was being optimistic, and that was cause for worry. "Gentlemen," he said, "I need those ships."

"And you shall have them," Worf told him.

Unfounded optimism and promises that might never be kept.

"I'm going to gather and organize the Starfleet squadrons as quietly as possible," Sisko told them. "I doubt there's a way to keep such maneuvers completely secret, but we're going to put off the Dominion's finding out about it as long as possible. We still have to move fast. I'll do my part here. You convince the chancellor to go along with me, and I'll get you both season tickets to the biggest game this side of Alpha Centauri."

"Security to Captain Sisko."

He motioned to the Klingons, then tapped his comm. "Sisko."

"Sir, we've got a citizen here who wants to talk to you, and only you."

"What about?"

"He won't say, sir. But he insists he broke through the lines at the Bajoran front on some kind of hardship pass. I tried to get him to leave and go through channels, but he's . . . kind of on the big side. Unless you want to see him, I'll have to call for backup to move him out of here."

Sisko looked at Worf, then Martok.

"Send him in, Ensign. Let's have a look."

Sisko spiraled into Admiral Ross's office without even announcing himself. Luckily, adjutants could get away with that from time to time. Well, once.

"Admiral, we've got a problem," he said before the door had managed to close behind him.

Ross looked up. "What kind of problem?"

"The kind that's going to make us move a lot earlier than makes any sense."

He held out an iridescent strip with a message encrypted on the dull side.

"You're condemning us with a Christmas ribbon?" Ross grumbled.

"It's not a Christmas ribbon. It's a birthday ribbon."

"Oh . . . happy birthday." Ross took the ribbon

and squinted at the message. "Minefield down stardate 69923.2 . . . station shields converted to gravity . . . grav—"

"Graviton emitter, sir. Dukat's people have figured out how to use the station to shut down the mines' replication system."

"Hell . . . are you sure this is reliable?"

"I've known the courier for five years. I trust him."

"Then we have a problem. According to this, the minefield's coming down in three days. The Ninth Fleet won't be here for at least four!"

Sisko steeled himself. This was the hard part.

"Then I suggest we go without them."

Ross visibly flinched at that idea, but clearly he'd seen it coming. "What about the Klingons?"

"Looks like we go without them too. We've run out of time, Admiral."

Too smart to argue that they shouldn't go, Ross sighed and nodded. "If those Dominion reinforcements come through the wormhole, we'll have lost everything. Okay, I can tell you've got an idea, so let's just hear it right now before my knees start shaking and I realize my son's on a ship docked right outside this starbase."

"We take the ships we have," Sisko said instantly, "fight our way to *Deep Space Nine,* and destroy that antigraviton emitter. It's our only hope."

They both hesitated then. Both looked at the little ribbon which changed everything.

With typical common sense and low-key decisiveness, Ross looked up at him without really moving. "Do it."

Sisko clutched his hand so tightly that the ribbon was half crushed. "Thank you, sir."

Bobbing his brows, Ross asked, "Well, aren't you going to mention the other thing?"

"Other thing, sir?"

"Well, sure."

"I . . ."

"You know, the thing that's been cooking on the back burner since you saw Dax put that phaser canister on the rack."

Feeling the blood rise to his face, Sisko was glad his complexion was dark enough to hide a blush.

Ross took the shiny ribbon from him, straightened it, then wrapped it around Sisko's wrist and tied a festive double bow. "There. Take yourself over to the *Defiant* and tell 'em you're a birthday present from Uncle Admiral. You've got your ship back. Now go get your station."

"Captain on the bridge."

Sisko was cheered by Nog's vaulting voice racing through the bridge as he stepped back into his command arena. From the rail, Bashir watched him, smiling. Over at engineering, O'Brien was trying not to smile. Failing, though. Nog looking good in his new ensign uniform—all was well in one little corner of the galaxy.

Dax floated out of the command chair, then turned the chair toward him. "I've kept it warm for you, Ben."

So much for ceremony. This felt good! No awkward transitions. Just come back and sit down. One thing goes right. One down, ten thousand to go.

"Ensign," Sisko said, tasting his first order in a while, "alert all ships. We're moving out."

A small set of words, not much that history would remember. Not exactly "Remember the Bismarck" or "I have not yet begun to fight." Small words, but enough to set into motion one of the largest task forces ever.

Even without the Ninth Fleet and without the Klingons, the gathered Starfleet ships and the ragtag Klingon bird of prey who had managed to muster at Starbase 375 were an impressive sight as they washed away from the silver spool of the base and flocked into the shimmering eternal night. Flanks of fighter ships and Klingon warbirds, columns of Starfleet support-tenders and power-packed frigates, progressing back to ships of the line, and finally a prancing troupe of picket destroyers—all led by the stubborn little knot of the *Defiant*. Sisko was proud to be leading them. Indeed, as victorious as this moment should be, he was instead deeply humbled and cold to the fingers with trepidation of what was to come. As majestic as this fleet indeed was, they simply didn't have enough ships to do the job.

Other things would have to come into play, things he had no control over. Like luck and chance and guesswork and the unlikely miracle that surprise would still be on their side when they fell out of warp at Bajor.

Those, and the faintest possibility that Kira and Odo and whoever else had sent him the message about the minefield's ticking clock would also be working against the Dominion inside the station. He hoped they knew he would come, because that would make them brave and they would take chances.

He would have to be ready, and make his crew ready, to jump at any chance they provided, or none if none came.

"Our initial intelligence reports have been verified. The Federation fleet is on the move."

Gul Dukat found a sour taste in his mouth as he reported the unsavory news to Weyoun. Deliberately he did not tack on what else he knew, until Weyoun asked.

"Do we know their destination?"

More sourness. "It would appear they're headed here."

"Here?" Weyoun paused, thought, then actually smiled with realization. "He knows we're taking down the minefield!" Then the smile dropped. "Someone must've gotten a message out."

"So it would seem."

"No matter," the Vorta tossed off. "We'll crush them."

"Yes, we will." Dukat handed him a padd with the significant information upon it. "And in order to do that, we're going to have to pull a significant number of our ships off the front lines."

"Do it."

Annoyance rumbled in Dukat's throat. Do it? That was all? Pull strategically arranged vessels to a central location, and the Vorta could see no problems with that kind of necessity?

"Once the minefield comes down," the Vorta was musing on, "there'll be more than enough ships to take their place."

"I understand," Dukat said, floating an impatient nod to Weyoun as Damar entered and took his attention. "One moment."

Damar stalked to him and instantly said, "I want your permission to arrest Major Kira."

"Kira?" Dukat lowered his voice. "What about Ziyal? Did you talk to her?"

"She doesn't want to see you. When I insisted, the major 'objected.'"

Suddenly boiling, Dukat glanced at Weyoun and forced some internal control. He knew by Damar's demeanor what had happened. He saw Kira's objection all over the bruised left side of Damar's face. "What did you do to Ziyal?"

"I did nothing to her," Damar quickly said.

"Then why did Kira attack you? You must've done something—threatened my daughter in some way. I *told* you to be tactful."

"Excuse me," Weyoun spoke up. "But don't you think resolving family squabbles can wait until after we've won this war?"

Annoyed first that Weyoun had heard them whispering and second that Weyoun could so easily trivialize the personal troubles weighing upon the leader of the Cardassian forces in this area, Dukat glared at him.

"Weak eyes," Weyoun said, "but good ears."

Nauseating.

"Yes," Dukat droned, "you're quite right."

"Then you're clear on what must be done."

"We will call back enough ships to destroy the Federation fleet and hold this station."

Like some kind of schoolchild reciting a rhyme.

Damar stiffened. "The Federation is moving against us?"

"That's right," Dukat told him. "Now, I want to hear exactly what went on between you and Ziyal."

"I tried to convince her to speak to you. She refused, and I took her arm. Kira struck out at me. When did you find out about the Federation? Have they discovered what we're doing with the antigraviton beam?"

"It seems so or they would not likely be moving so near our bringing down the minefield. Was Ziyal upset?"

"I don't know. Is Captain Sisko leading the fleet himself?"

"We have no information about that. Pay attention, Damar—was Ziyal angry at me?"

"She was . . . she was disturbed. I'm sure it'll work out. Fathers and daughters—families—these things happen, sir. But the Federation—"

"Will get here in its own time. When it comes, we will smash it. I want my daughter at my side, Damar . . . that was *your* job."

Damar's face hardened. "I resist this expectation you have that I can manage your daughter!"

"I do, too." Weyoun stood up and faced them both. "It is inappropriate for you to concern yourself, Dukat, with the irritations of personal problems when larger things are looming."

Flaring, Damar knotted his fists. "I need no assistance from such as you, Vorta!"

Instantly Dukat pressed a hand to Damar's chest and pushed him back. This was a deadly road. The Vorta, however cloying and disgusting, was immensely powerful in his attachment to the Founders, and Damar represented the Cardassian presence. For Weyoun to sense a flaw in the armor of Cardassia could be a virus in Dukat's long-term plans for his own empire.

"So much passion," Dukat uttered, bottling his own furious tension. "I am honored, both of you. Yes, of course I will attend the coming invasion. Damar, take your place in Ops. We must cap any venom that flows through the veins of our victory. You and I will review the repairs on the station. We must make many plans. We're going into battle. We must have order . . . there must be order here . . . and goodwill among us . . . You see, we must somehow fight . . . be a unit, one and all . . . and at the same time we must bring down the minefield."

He turned to Weyoun.

"As promised."

"Major!"

She heard him call.

She ignored him.

Too much to do, too many fronts to cover—a hundred worries, and only two hands . . . the turbolift closed on the echo of his call.

The station seemed so quiet. Only the whir of the lift.

Several decks down, the lift breathed to a stop and the doors opened. And she still heard him call.

"Kira!"

He came around the far corner. Must've come down another lift.

She turned away and hurried to her tasks.

Behind her, Odo's soft boots thumped on the deck carpet. "Wait, please—"

"I have nothing to say to you," she said, and meant it.

"I understand you're angry."

"You bet I'm angry." At this she stopped and spun

to face him. "Do you have any idea what's been going on all this time while you've been locked in your private world with that . . . that pseudo-woman?"

"Yes, somewhat," he said with undenied sheepishness. "I've been occupied."

Through her teeth she burned, "Dukat's bringing down the minefield, the Federation is about to be overrun by Dominion forces, and Weyoun's ordered Rom's execution. And you've been 'occupied.'"

She whirled around and paced away, leaving him to catch up. "It's so difficult to explain—"

"If you're going to tell me about the link, don't bother," she told him. "I'm a 'solid,' remember? I wouldn't understand."

"Nerys—" He caught her arm, and she felt herself draw up short. "I'm sorry."

"Sorry? That's what you wanted to say to me? You're sorry?"

"Yes . . ."

"Let me tell you something, Odo, we are way past 'sorry.'"

"I heard you got a message out to Captain Sisko."

"How did you hear that?"

"Jake told me."

"Jake's foolish to speak to you while that woman is still around here."

He looked as hurt as he ever had. "You don't trust me?"

She felt her eyes flare and her blunt honesty shoot

out. "Would *you* trust you? I don't know what kind
of influence she's had over you for all these days. By
your own admission, you don't know whether or not
she knows what you know after one of those moult-
ing sessions."

"Melding . . ."

"You call it anything you want. All I know is that I
have no way to be sure she isn't manipulating you,
Odo. You're a strong person with flawless convic-
tions and you're as brave as anyone I've ever known,
except when this shapeshifter persona comes over
you. Then you . . . you change. And I don't mean
physically. We're going into a deadly few hours and
you haven't been here for the important parts. You
haven't shared the tension and the fear and the
worry. For that, you can bet your 'sorry' will never
be enough. For the rest of it, I'm going to do
everything I can to deprive the Dominion of this
station and Dukat of the glory and Weyoun of Rom's
death. You can go back with her or you can join us.
But you cannot do both. That part, Odo, is over.
Make up your mind who you are and quit letting
somebody else tell you. If you want to be one of us
again, understand that you're damned right along
with us. Otherwise, you go with her, and be damned
alone."

When can their glory fade?
O the wild charge they made!

CHAPTER 13

A BEAUTIFUL AND terrifying sight, indeed, was the Starfleet combined armada, sailing across open space in a silent tapestry of constructed wonder. Slightly less than six hundred ships. Five hundred ninety-two, at latest count.

Still, even as Ben Sisko marveled at the beauty of so many ships gathered here, he knew they were less than a third of what they might have been if only time had allowed the gathering of power. If only the Klingons had been able to get here in time, if only the Ninth and Second Fleets had been able to make it here in time.

But there were positives too—a smaller armada drew less attention.

Sisko frowned at himself. There had to be more positives than that, didn't there?

And there were troubles. Many of these ships were still handling damage. The *Defiant* herself had not been soundly repaired from her last four missions, but just had patches piled on jury-rigs on improvisations and now she was flying again. Nearby, in comforting proximity, was the *Centaur,* brimming with Charlie Reynolds's tough little crew, and *Rotarran,* and other individual ships which had performed so nobly in the past few weeks. He wanted to contact them and tell them how glad he was that they were so close, and all about to go into the strife at one another's side, yet he restrained himself. Unnecessary, sentimental ship-to-ship communications would be unwise, and this was a time for stiff wisdom. Others were conspicuously and painfully missing. *Lyric, K'lashm'a,* and the *Traynor* were all destroyed lately in action, and Sisko felt their absence like a keen blade nicking the corner of his heart. Bitterness welled, and he fought it all the way. Until the war came, his world had been the station of DS9 and the crew of the *Defiant,* but little more. Now there was more, and he wanted it all.

"Sir."

Dax at the helm, O'Brien and Nog at engineering and tactical stations, Garak at the science station— he'd pretty much earned a position . . . Bashir right here at Sisko's side—

"Sir."

Sisko turned—O'Brien was speaking to him.

"Incoming message from the *Cortez*," the chief said. "They're still having trouble stabilizing the guidance thrusters on their port nacelle."

"Tell them to drop back and make repairs. Bring up the *Sarek* to take its place."

"Will do."

Gloomy at this news, Garak looked up. "That's the eleventh ship to fall out of formation."

"Nice of you to keep track, Garak," Dax scolded.

"He can't help being negative," Bashir said. "It's his nature."

"On the contrary," Garak retorted, "I always hope for the best. Unfortunately, experience has taught me to expect the worst."

"I'm picking something up." O'Brien's announcement clicked them all back to work. "Sir, it's a large Dominion fleet, bearing zero-zero-zero mark zero-zero-nine!"

Sisko watched the helm monitors, but nothing showed yet. "How large?"

O'Brien checked his sensors, then checked them again. His face drained of half its color.

"Twelve hundred and fifty-four ships."

Sisko's head pounded. The Dominion must have found out they were coming and gathered up. Beside his shoulder, Bashir's voice was ill wind. "They outnumber us two to one . . ."

Garak smiled snidely. "Now who's being negative?"

"On screen," Sisko ordered, "maximum magnification."

With the ship's sensors pulling for all they were worth, a wide-scan view came into focus on the main screen and several diagnostic monitors. Before them lay a cargo net of enemy ships, sprawled in a great dotted curtain against space, backlit by the warm and strangely welcoming Bajoran sun.

"Ship to ship," Sisko ordered. Then he didn't wait. He tapped the comm himself. "To all ships . . . this is Captain Sisko. Assume attack formation Delta-2. Cruiser and Galaxy wings, drop to half impulse. You too, Dax."

"Half impulse."

Garak glanced at his science board, but this wasn't exactly a survey mission. "I feel sorry for the Klingons. They're going to miss a very interesting fight."

Without looking up, O'Brien commented, "I have a feeling we're going to miss having them here."

"Forget the Klingons," Sisko coldly told them. "Our job is to get to *Deep Space Nine* and prevent the Dominion reinforcements from coming through the wormhole. And that's what we're going to do. Attack fighters, tactical pattern Theta. Concentrate your fire on the Cardassian ships, then split off into squadrons and run like hell."

With an attack order, the *Defiant* automatically went to red alert, as if life's blood were suddenly flowing through the ship and her crew and mingling between them.

He knew the last order might be confusing, but there was no time nor any inclination, as tactical group leader, to explain his hopes to get the Cardassians angry enough to break formation and follow the running Federation fighters.

There would be no such chance with the by-the-book Jem'Hadar, who couldn't be baited. But the Cardassians—they might provide a hole to punch through.

"Attack fighters, prepare to engage on my command." Sisko leaned back in his chair as the armada dropped out of warp. "There's an old saying . . . 'Fortune favors the bold.' Well, we're about to find out."

Noble six hundred!

CHAPTER

14

"ATTACK FIGHTERS, full impulse and fire at will."

Sisko waited until the last possible moment, calculating distance, trajectory, breadth of energy wash, fallout, and weapons and fuel limitations, then gave the order to open fire.

He was one second too late. The Dominion fleet opened fire first and got in the critical initial hits, blowing back several of the Federation fighters' first wave in such a flurry that there was no way to visually count the casualties. The remaining fighters unleashed a barrage of quantum torpedoes at the center of the Dominion curtain. Sisko flinched to see several of them immediately destroyed, but was heartened as the rest followed Sisko's plan and broke formation, then split in four directions.

Sisko stood up on braced legs and watched.

"They're not taking the bait," O'Brien voiced.

"Ensign," Sisko said to Nog, "send in the second wave. Tell them to keep targeting the Cardassians."

"Aye, sir. Second wave on its way . . . third and fourth waves on hot-standby."

To O'Brien, Sisko ordered, "Have Destroyer Wings two and six move in closer. They need more cover fire. And tell Captains Diego and Reynolds to stay alert. They may try to outflank us."

That man talking sure sounded like he knew what he was doing. Sisko buried his nervousness in a long breath and held it several seconds. In fact, he had never done this, never choreographed a multisquadron maneuver of any kind. One station, one ship—oddly enough, this was a lot more like running the station than running a ship. Still, how many things was he doing wrong? He had never been a commodore before. This was a hell of a way to start—four hundred vessels waiting for him to tell them which part of the stage to dance on . . .

Trying to trick the enemy into cracking open their own lines—it had seemed good when he first thought of it, but he realized now that he had been relying too much on training. This was one of the primary battle maneuvers. Where did he get the idea that Dukat wouldn't know about it or expect it?

Dukat would know that the station's deflector grid that would drag down the minefield, and not the ships defending it, would be the Federation fleet's target. He would send wave after wave of fighters, if he had to. He would regroup and send fighters who had already gone. If Dukat could not be tempted, perhaps the Cardassian commanders of individual ships could be angered to madness. Maybe.

Then what? What if a hole did open up? Knowing that Dukat understood this maneuver, what should the Federation forces do if Dukat let them have their way?

Suddenly very insecure and sharply suspicious of his own plans, Sisko scrambled in his mind to come up with a half-dozen alternate plans for whatever happened next.

The problem was, he had no idea what might happen next.

"Sisko is trying to provoke us into opening a hole in our lines. He's determined to get here and stop us from taking down the minefield. I plan to give Sisko his opening . . . and then close it on him."

Dukat's mind nearly wandered toward the flicker of victory he saw swimming around before his imagination, but at his sides reality shifted. Weyoun on one side, the female shapeshifter on the other, and Damar over there, all watching the computer graphic schematic of the battle unfolding on their perimeter.

"Proceed," the female deigned.

A terrible tightness ran up the backs of Dukat's legs. *Proceed* . . . He gritted his teeth and held back from comment. *His* was the final word. *He* was in command here.

Proceed. Pruuuu ceeeed.

"Tonight," Dukat told them, "we will drink to the conquerors of the Federation. I've waited a long time for this."

"Aren't you being premature?" Weyoun pointed out.

"I don't think so. Not with twenty-eight hundred Dominion ships about to come through the wormhole and reinforce us."

"What about the minefield?" Weyoun asked. "Are we still on schedule?"

Forcing himself back to the moment, Dukat ground out, "We should be able to detonate the mines in eight hours."

"Good," the female said.

Why didn't she melt back into a pot somewhere?

Luckily, she decided for some undisclosed reason to turn and leave. Perhaps the presence of people with actual backbones was repugnant to her. Good.

"Eight hours," Weyoun echoed. "I'll hold you to that, Dukat. A lot can happen in that time."

"Tell me, Weyoun, have you ever been diagnosed as anhedonic?"

Weyoun's black eyes hardened. "You think I'm incapable of joy just because I'm being cautious?"

"We didn't defeat the Federation by being cautious."

"We haven't defeated them yet. And even if we do, that's only the beginning. Holding on to a prize as vast as the Federation isn't going to be easy. It's going to require an enormous number of ships, a massive occupation army, and constant vigilance."

From somewhere in the bowels of determination, Dukat scoured up a smile. "I'm looking forward to it."

"I'm sure you're also looking forward to occupying Bajor. And we all know what a disappointment that was for you."

"On Bajor," Dukat shot back, too defensively to hide, "I merely implemented policy. I didn't make it. If I had, things would've turned out quite differently."

"If you ask me," the damned Vorta pressed, "the key to holding the Federation is Earth. If there's going to be an organized resistance against us, its birthplace will be there."

"You could be right."

"Then our first step will be to eradicate its population. It's the only way."

Dukat stared at him. Admittedly, this revelation was shocking. Control had always been the Cardassian way. Eradication—that was another color of flag completely.

"You can't do that," he attempted.

Weyoun's sanctimonious brows went up. "Why not?"

"Because a true victory is to make your enemy see that they were wrong to oppose you in the first place. To force them to acknowledge your greatness—"

"Then you kill them?" The brows stayed up.

"Only if necessary."

Weyoun murmured something else, but Dukat didn't hear it.

Instead he drifted into a foggy thought, lingering for a moment in the distant past as he gazed at the graphic of the battle so nearby.

"Perhaps," he uttered, "the biggest disappointment of my life is that the Bajoran people still refuse to appreciate how lucky they were to have me as their liberator. I protected them in so many ways . . . cared for them as if they were my own children . . . but to this day, is there a single statue of me on Bajor?"

"I would guess not," Weyoun said. He needn't have said anything. He just wanted to hear his own voice making noise.

"And you'd be right," Dukat sighed. He looked down at his hand—in it was the baseball he had been clutching all day. He'd forgotten it was there. "Take Captain Sisko . . . an otherwise intelligent and perceptive man . . . even he refuses to grant me the respect I deserve. You find that amusing?"

"Not at all. I find it fascinating."

"Laugh all you want. History will prove me right."

Weyoun offered only a simpering grin. "I can hardly wait."

After securing the last word, which was apparently the only reason Weyoun ever spoke once a subject was exhausted, the Vorta floated around and followed his Founder-god out of the operations area.

Arrogance and threats. Dukat's hands shook and he hid them under the edge of the graphic panels.

Damar stewed beside him. "I'd like to toss that smug little Vorta out the nearest airlock and his Founder with him."

Ah, focus.

Dukat forced his neck to relax. He still had an image to maintain.

"Now, Damar. That's no way to talk about our valued allies. Not until this war is over, anyway."

Visibly controlling himself, Damar turned to him. "Sir, there is one other thing."

"Make it brief."

"I'm concerned about further attempts to sabotage this station. The enemy knows that if they don't act soon, it'll be too late."

"By 'enemy,' I assume you're referring to Rom's associates?"

Damar nodded. "I doubt he was working alone when he tried to sabotage the station. He must've had help. His wife Leeta, Jake Sisko, Major Kira—"

"What are you proposing?"

"That we arrest them and keep them in custody, at least until the wormhole is reopened."

His innards grating, Dukat felt the pull of everything to which he was obliged. "A wise precaution, but our Bajoran 'allies' might object to an arrest without cause. If anyone asks, we're merely holding them for questioning. And Damar . . . make sure they're not harmed in *any* way. Major Kira is very important to my daughter. And to me."

At mention of this delicacy, Damar hesitated. "Sir, about your daughter . . . perhaps it would be better, for her own sake, if Ziyal were confined to quarters."

Dukat hardened instantly. "For what reason?"

"To be perfectly honest, sir, I don't completely trust her. And neither should you."

The boldness beneath Damar's hesitation gave Dukat a chill.

"Are you accusing my daughter of being a saboteur?"

"I'm not accusing her of anything," Damar said quickly, "but she is quite friendly with Major Kira—"

"That will be all, Damar."

"She doesn't appreciate what it means to be Cardassian! Or to be your daughter!"

"But she *is* my daughter." Dukat pivoted to glare directly into Damar's steel eyes and meet them with the acid of his own. "That may mean nothing to you, but it means everything to me. Perhaps you can overlook that, but I can't."

The graphic screen beside them flickered. Things were happening outside. Things were changing. Things were dangerous, volatile, unpredictable.

And in here, things were cold. Very cold . . . very cold.

Minefields, forcefields, multiphasic how-to-shut'em-down fields—Kira's mind roiled with fields and forces and molecular disruption as she sat at a sheltered corner table in Quark's nearly empty bar. Jake sat with her, and across from them was a nervous Leeta. Hovering over and trying to appear busy, Quark held an empty tray.

"I heard that the Federation fleet has been ambushed," Leeta fished.

Quark wasn't helping. "I heard two Cardassian soldiers saying the fleet was completely destroyed."

As Kira shot him a glare for his indiscreet gossiping, Jake Sisko, the Great Journalist, said, "Don't believe everything you hear."

"Jake's right," Kira pounced. "Sisko'll be here. The questions is, will he get here in time."

"He's only got seven hours before they detonate the minefield and start bringing reinforcements through the wormhole."

Jake narrowed his eyes. "We've got to stop them."

"How?" Leeta sensibly asked, but with a jagged edge of hopelessness. Sisko's limited hours were also theirs.

Kira noticed that all their eyes quite abruptly swung on her. So she tossed out the thoughts she'd been turning. "What if we cut the power supply to the main computer? Shut down the whole station."

"Great," Quark snarled. "That'll put me out of business altogether."

"It'll also keep them from detonating the mines."

"Okay, so we shut down the main computer. How?"

Kira shrugged. "With a bomb."

"What kind of bomb?"

"Leave that to me." A simple way of saying she had no idea. "It'll be crude, but effective."

Quark shook his head. For all his eternal pessimism about anything that upset the status quo, he had a streak of sensibleness that made Kira look up and pay attention as he said, "The main computer's in the central core. It's too heavily guarded. You'll never be able to smuggle a bomb in there."

With that blunt—and quite correct—declaration, he noticed the wandering eyes of a Jem'Hadar who walked by the bar entrance and Quark too walked away from the table, making their meeting seem less conspiratorial.

Kira appreciated the simple but critical move. She knew Quark wanted to be here, not over there.

But bundling was bad strategy. Even if they weren't plotting sabotage, it was a better idea to avoid clustering.

She spoke quietly, but was careful with her expression. "I'll plant the bomb . . . all we need to do is distract the guards."

"Ah, Major—there you are."

Damar. With two Cardassian soldiers. Maybe

Quark had moved away because he saw them coming.

The Cardassians approached the table and Damar grinned mirthlessly.

"How nice of you to gather your friends for us," he said immediately to Kira.

"I'm off duty, Damar," she returned. "What do you want?"

"I want you to come with me. All three of you."

Kira looked up sharply. "Where?"

"To the security office. We have some questions to ask you."

Jake Sisko stiffened visibly. "What kind of questions?"

"You'll find out when we get there."

Instantly, instinctively, Kira sized up the Cardassians for a sprint escape. An uppercut could dispatch Damar. One of the guards could be smashed in the face by Damar's knobby skull if she hit them with enough force—

"Go ahead, Major," Damar invited. "Nothing would make me happier."

As he spoke, two more Cardassian guards appeared at the doorway.

The odds of fighting their way out dissolved. She might make it alone, but Jake and Leeta . . . oh, who was she kidding? She couldn't even make it alone.

"Don't worry," she told them as she rose to her feet. "It'll be all right."

"Of course it will," Damar said. "You have nothing to hide, do you? You certainly don't."

For an instant, Kira thought he might be satisfied if she went with him alone, but Damar lagged back until Jake and Leeta stood also and were herded out by the guards. She caught Quark's lonely gaze in her periphery on the way out, and prayed he wouldn't speak up. If this was it, if they were out of commission, Quark was the last of their meager hopes.

Uh-oh . . .

"Captain, two squadrons of Cardassian attack ships are breaking formation! They're going after our fighters!"

Miles O'Brien's victorious report comforted Ben Sisko none at all. He had sent nine waves of fighters at the wall of Dominion ships. They had complied with his plans. Now he was really worried.

"We've opened a hole in their lines," Garak uttered with undue admiration.

Sisko looked at the panels. "Have we?"

Dax nodded. "Sir, do you see those Galor-class destroyers?"

"I see them."

Then Bashir confirmed everything that had been worrying Sisko by saying, "It's a trap . . ."

Sisko felt his stomach tighten.

"It's also an opportunity. And we may not get another. Ensign, have Galaxy wings nine-one and nine-three engage those destroyers. All other ships, head for that opening. Anyone who gets through doesn't stop until they reach *Deep Space Nine*."

In spear formation, with the *Defiant* as the point, *Centaur* and *Sarek* anchoring the corners, the Federation squadron blared forward toward the hole in the Dominion lines, firing all the way. The enemy fleet unleashed its own weapons and cut wounds into the Federation flanks even before the hole was breached. With the ships tightening formation, almost every shot from both sides found a target.

But the hole certainly would be breached. The cost was already enormous—casualty after casualty fell from the Federation formation, quick to get out of the way after suffering too much damage to keep going. That was a good plan—get out of the way, don't tempt other allied vessels to render assistance. Leave the path clear. Other ships tightened the lines to take their places, and Sisko was proud to a point of being choked up when he saw that the Starfleet captains were freely sacrificing themselves in order that the *Defiant* and the lead ships should break through. Captains had egos, to be sure, and they were all compromising themselves in order to let Ben Sisko be the one to breach the line. The generosity of it overwhelmed him. Even more stunning was the evil relief he felt when he saw that Charlie Reynolds was still with him and not among the casualties.

Terrible, ungentlemanly—to pick and choose who he wanted to survive, to have preferences or wishes like that. He had always wanted to be above that sort of thing, but what could a man do? The only way to care unilaterally about everyone in general was to avoid caring about anyone in particular, and he just couldn't do that. Not perfect, apparently.

The terrifying proximity slammed home and drove Sisko out of his personal thoughts as enemy fire rocked the *Defiant* with a deafening boom. He turned to see if Dax were going to return fire, if she even had a clear shot, but on the substation's monitor at engineering he saw the *Centaur* open up on the Jem'Hadar ship that had hit *Defiant* and drive it off the attack course.

"Congratulations, Captain," Garak spoke up. "You wanted them angry. They're angry."

"The *Magellan* and the *Venture* are supposed to be protecting our starboard flank," Sisko observed, "but they're in too tight. Ensign, tell the Sixth, Seventh, and Eighth Fighter Squadrons to regroup and—"

"Sir, I can't get through to anybody! Communications are down!"

So much for the commodore's choreography.

"They're jamming our signals by generating a rotating EM pulse," O'Brien explained.

"Can you clear it?"

"I'm trying to."

As they spoke, hit after hit rocked the ship despite the protection of several other vessels around them, and on two of the port screens Sisko clearly saw the

Centaur dive aside as *Argent Wing* and the *Admiral Stanley* were both pummeled to bits no bigger than soupbowls. Some of the power surges they were feeling were the wash from utter destruction of their comrades.

He watched and held his breath as *Centaur* spun on its starboard side, wheeled belly-up, then continued its roll and righted herself on the assault plane, but now had fallen out of protective formation. Sisko parted his lips—wanted to call over there and ask Charlie his condition.

No, no, this wasn't the time for that. Not until—

Half the bridge erupted into smoke and sparks so thick that Sisko couldn't tell where the damage had occurred. Two crewmen went down on the deck—one got back up. On the screen, the *Sitak* spun out of control. Beyond them, a ship Sisko didn't recognize took a hard direct hit and veered off.

"Sir," Dax shouted over the crackle, "we've just lost the *Sitak* and the *Majestic*. We're on our own, Ben!"

"Comm's back on line!" O'Brien called.

From Nog—"Four enemy ships dead ahead!"

"Evasive maneuvers," Sisko called, "pattern Omega. We're going through!"

"Forward, the Light Brigade!
Charge for the guns!" he said.

CHAPTER
15

"COME ON, ROGER, plow the way for him! Heading three-three-nine-zero right now, Randy boy, right now!"

Charlie Reynolds roared his orders with a lilt of winning possibility. There was the golden prize, right there, the way through to *Deep Space Nine,* the Federation's chance to botch all the Dominion's cancerous plans and negate all their back-wins, if only Sisko and the *Defiant* could shear through there.

"Protect him! Fire on those pursuing ships!"

Engineer Fitzgerald turned and paused in his work for an almost casual moment. "You don't want me to repair main drive long-range thrust? Try to get us through there with him?"

"Hell, yes, try to get us through! If anybody gets through to *Deep Space Nine,* I sure as hell want to be one of 'em! What's the leak situation, Fitz?"

"Bad. Plasma."

"Plug it and keep the shields up. Get ready to shift 'em aft if we clear the Dominion lines."

"We're going through!" Roger Buick cheered, working his helm like a charging horse. "Great!"

The lilt in his navigator's voice made Reynolds realize he'd made a mistake. "Stay behind *Defiant,*" he corrected instantly. "We'll go through, but Sisko deserves to go in first and show those Cardassians how the bread's buttered."

"What, and we don't?" Lang complained without taking his eyes off the nav and weapons station.

"Ten points starboard, and shut up, Randy."

"Right."

"More speed, Fitz. Let's tease one of those bastards off *Defiant* if we can."

The *Centaur* sucked its way into a tight turn and trailed a beautiful glittering stream of plasma leakage as it roared forward and opened fire on the ships pursuing Sisko.

There it was—a break in Dominion lines. And there was the *Defiant,* surging ahead, crackling with bright damage, making for the breach in the enemy line. *Centaur* raced forward at a ridiculous speed for close combat, blowing past two of the five vessels pursuing Sisko, firing all the way. Charlie could feel the taste of burning metal in his mouth. All he wanted was a bite off one Jem'Hadar tail section.

"Come on, I just want one of them off him! Veer starboard! Ram it if you have to!"

Nobody questioned the order. They just held on tight as Randy Lang slammed the ship sideways and drove its starboard wing into the port engine strut of the nearest Jem'Hadar ship.

Instantly that ship was forced out of the line of pursuit. Locked together like rutting stags, the two ships wheeled on a diagonal across the path toward the break in Dominion lines, and lost the course.

"Break us off him!" Charlie shouted. "Hard over! Shake 'im off!"

No one responded, but he saw his helmsman's shoulders working, and at the best moment Fitzgerald hammered his board and jettisoned several hull plates on that side, causing the two ships to slide off each other.

That was when the Jem'Hadar ship turned on them without losing any speed at all. Uh-oh— Charlie suddenly realized he should've kept a grip on the tiger's tail while he had it. Now the tiger was turning.

Before he could take a breath the enemy ship opened fire at point-blank range. *Centaur* bucked like a convulsing animal.

"Shields are down!" Gerrie Ruddy gulped suddenly. "We just lost the whole grid, Charlie!"

"He's on our tail!" Buick shouted at the same time. "Coming through the plasma stream!"

"Can we increase speed?"

"I'm full-out now!"

"Fire on them."

"Too much drain," Fitzgerald cryptically said. "Phasers are down seventy percent."

As a cold wash engulfed his body under the film of sweat, Reynolds turned to the aft-view screen and looked at the face of slaughter plowing toward them. No shields . . . no shields.

The faces of his crew turned to him as meadow flowers turn in a wind.

"Fire aft with whatever you've got," Charlie ordered. His voice drummed in his ears. "Hurt him if you can. Keep punching until the last moment. Sisko's getting through. We won. This is it. Gerry, release the destruct log buoy. Fitz, emergency breaking thrusters in five seconds. If we gotta go, we're taking those bastards with us."

With four enemy fighters in hot pursuit, the *Defiant* raced on a direct spinning path straight through the break in Dominion lines, taking every hit with stalwart will and good old-fashioned hard-shelled hull plates. With so many shields down or flickering, the plain shell of the plates was all that stood between the crew and very quick death.

"That's one down!" Dax called as the *Defiant*

successfully drilled the nearest Jem'Hadar ship into Swiss cheese and forced it to fall out of pursuit.

"Can you shake the other three?" Sisko asked her.

"I'm trying."

Of course she was trying. Why did he ask the obvious at times like this? Bad habit.

"We've lost aft shields," a sweaty Bashir reported. "Forward shields are down to twenty percent."

"This might be a good time to cloak," Garak suggested.

"The cloaking system's fried," O'Brien instantly said.

Sisko turned. "Divert auxiliary power to weapons. Let's see if we can fight our way out of this."

The beetlelike Jem'Hadar pursuit ships bore down on them. They must be sacrificing everything to speed and weapons. Sisko felt his chest constrict. *Defiant,* in this condition, couldn't afford to flush everything to speed, and weapons would never be enough to take out three of those hard-nail fighters.

Suddenly the whole ship was pushed from behind—not a hit, but something else. A stern wash of some kind, like an ocean wave hitting a surfboard. Sisko looked around . . . no damage reports coming up . . . what was that?

Rather than ask for something his crew would tell him as soon as they knew it, he clamped his lips and forced himself to wait.

The viewscreen flickered—Nog said something,

but over the crackle of his panel, his words were lost. Something about being hailed—

"On screen," Sisko told him. Might as well talk to whoever was hailing.

The comm screen zapped a few times, then tried to focus on a face.

"Sorry we're late, Captain, but it wasn't easy to convince Chancellor Gowron to spare us any ships."

Sisko felt the blood drain out of his throbbing head. Worf! He'd completely forgotten about the Klingons!

"Just glad you could join us, Commander," he responded, barely hearing his own voice.

"Captain," O'Brien interrupted, "the Klingons have opened a hole in the Dominion lines."

"Dax, can you take us through?"

"I'd love to try."

Leaving the Klingons to cover their stern, Sisko didn't bother with amenities that would only distract their saviors. On the screens he could clearly see the knot of dogfights going on as Klingon birds of prey and heavy cruisers flocked into the struggle and divided the Jem'Hadar pursuit ships among them like hounds ripping flesh from kicking prey. The tide had turned—

And the *Defiant* had a clear path through enemy lines and forward at high speed toward *Deep Space Nine*.

"Any other ships make it?" he asked.

"No, sir," Nog tightly answered.

Not much of a surprise there. All the other ships had worked to clear the way so he could get through, and he couldn't even call back a thank-you without distracting them from the terrible fight he was forced to leave behind.

As if his guts were being gored alive, he hated leaving them. Even running out for a good reason was running out—yet he knew they were fighting to buy him time to run.

"We've got three hours before the minefield is detonated," he murmured. "Set a course for *Deep Space Nine,* maximum warp."

"Maximum warp," Dax confirmed, then turned and gave him one of her typically soothing looks. "If I were you, I'd start coming up with plan B."

"The *Defiant* has broken through our lines." Damar's voice was gravelly as he stared at the reports coming through from the front. "It's on its way here. Shall I order pursuit?"

Gul Dukat parted his lips to answer, but it was Weyoun who spoke first.

"At once," the Vorta fluidly said.

Stiff and insulted, Dukat countermanded with a glance to Damar. "The *Defiant*'s no match for this station. If Sisko wants to commit suicide, I say we let him."

"Sir, the Klingons have outflanked us," Damar told him. "Our lines are beginning to crumble."

Dukat's hands grew cold again. He could no

longer feel the shape of the baseball he was holding. "There's nothing to worry about. Soon thousands of Dominion ships will start pouring through the wormhole. I just hope the *Defiant* gets here in time for Sisko to see it."

"How much longer before they detonate the minefield?" Rom asked.

Since Kira couldn't see him from this angle in her holding cell, she only sighed and grumbled, "I wish you'd stop asking me that."

"Sorry."

Sharing her cell, Leeta just shivered with dread. In the next cell, Rom and Jake also sat waiting for Armageddon.

Then Jake couldn't stand the silence and guessed, "I'd say about ninety minutes."

Rom sorrowfully muttered, "My time grows short."

"Don't say that!" his fiancée mourned.

"The only reason they haven't killed me yet is that I'm part of their victory celebration. Seven o'clock . . . Dukat makes a speech . . . eight-thirty, cake and raktajino . . . eight forty-five, execute the Ferengi."

Kira parted her lips to put a stop to that, but a voice from the outer cell area cut her off.

"Lunch for Major Kira."

Inside the holding cell, Kira straightened in her seat. That was Quark! He was speaking up more sharply than anyone needed to speak in the holding cell area. Quickly she motioned Leeta to be silent, not to react at all, or the two Jem'Hadar guards would, even in their lunkheadedness, be able to gauge that there was something stirring.

Kira hoped Jake and Rom, in the next cell, would have the sense to be quiet too. She tensed, but remained very still and listened.

"Major Kira has already been fed." That was the Cardassian warden.

"And I can only imagine," Quark's voice perked again, "the slop you've served her. What I have here is Hasperate soufflé. Just the way the major likes it."

"Do you know who I am?"

Another voice—Kira flinched to hear it. Ziyal!

"Gul Dukat's daughter," the warden acknowledged, but he wasn't impressed.

"That's right. Now I suggest you allow us to deliver this food."

As Kira strained to hear, there was a brief silence, then a shuffle of movement.

"I can't do that," the warden finally said. "However, I will take the tray to her. After I examine it."

"Is that really necessary?" Quark asked.

"Lift the lid."

"If you insist."

A scratch of metal . . .

"You see? Hasperate soufflé. Just as I said. Stop poking at it! It's very delicate—"

More sounds. A shuffle . . . a hiss . . . a splat . . .

Then Quark muttered something else. This time the Cardassian didn't answer.

There were more sounds of movement, then Quark suddenly appeared with a disruptor in each hand and Ziyal right behind him. They struck a ridiculous but somehow enheartening pose as Quark shouted at the two Jem'Hadar guards.

"All right! No one move!"

The Jem'Hadar stared at him, but didn't lower their weapons.

"Brother!" Rom gasped. "I knew you would come!"

"It's a surprise to me," Quark drawled.

He kept both disruptors pointed at the guards. Kira thought he looked nervous, as if he would rather be behind his bar and who could blame him, but the Jem'Hadar didn't seem to know how to judge the demeanor of a Ferengi. They still didn't move.

"Just keep calm and stay where you are," he said to the guards. "Understand? Don't move. You— open the holding cells." When the guards still didn't respond, Quark insisted, "I said open the holding cells!"

Ziyal glanced at him. "You told them not to move."

"Right. Nobody moves except you," Quark said, pointing at one of the guards. "Now open the cells."

The Jem'Hadar exchanged a quick glance of clean communication, then turned their weapons downward, but Quark, with the advantage of his nervousness, instantly fired. Both guards were struck in the chest, one a little more off center than the other, but well enough done.

Quark stood in a pool of astonishment, looking at the crumpled masses of what he had done. Two Jem'Hadar soldiers, all by himself.

"Quark," Kira murmured admiringly.

He was still staring at the bodies. "Yes?"

"Take down the forcefields."

"Forcefields?"

Still he didn't move. Ziyal moved to him, took one of the disruptors from his hand, went to the cell control panel, aimed, closed her eyes, and fired at the key pad.

The cell forcefields flashed, sizzled, and dissolved. Leeta rushed from her cell and into Rom's arms. Kira rushed out also and embraced one of the Jem'Hadar's rifles, then hurried to confiscate the other one, which she tossed to Rom. "We've got to find a way to shut down the power to the main computer!"

"I can do that," Rom quickly said.

Leeta gazed at him and looked as if she wanted to do something that didn't involve computers. "Oh, Rom . . ."

"That is," he considered, "if we can make it to the central computer core without being killed."

"Rom, you're with me!" Kira snapped them out of their respective, if not collaborating, thoughts. "The rest of you, find some place to keep out of sight!"

"Will do!" Jake called, urging Ziyal out to the corridor and dragging the still-stupefied Quark after them.

Kira led Rom in a charge out into the main corridor, but by then their biochemistry had triggered the scanner-sentry and the alarms were ringing. There was no stopping that, not in less than twenty minutes, anyway, and she wanted those minutes for something a lot more important than just avoiding a fight. Besides, if she and Rom attracted enough attention, Jake, Quark, and Leeta might find a sensor-shielded area to hide.

That was critical—if they were taken prisoner again, they could be used as leverage against Kira and Rom, and Kira knew she would find the resolve deep within herself to let them be casually killed by the angry Cardassians rather than let the whole Alpha Quadrant be risked. That was her duty, her moral obligation, and she had to be ready for it. If the entire station and everybody she had come to care about had to be sacrificed . . . she would do it.

In minutes they were being pursued by three Cardassian troops, but by now she had led Rom into the lower levels, into the cargo bays. Stacks of crates, boxes, shipping cartons, and cool metal kegs protected them from the wildfire from the furious Cardassians.

"This way!" she called to Rom, not bothering to waste rifle shots back the way they'd come.

When the doors at the opposite side of the bay,

right where she was headed, opened and discharged three Jem'Hadar soldiers, their weapons blazing even before they could possibly have clear shots, Kira had no choice but to shoot. She ducked behind a stack of cargo and fired, hoping to cover Rom in case he wasn't fast enough to take cover.

Slamming her shoulder hard into a storage bin, Kira tried to find a break in the enemy assault to shoot back, but the barrage was insane. Sparks and rattling disruptor fire chewed into the stack of cargo, blasting the crates and containers wide open, splintering her and Rom with shavings of hot metal and razor-edged shards of plastic. The stink almost choked her and made her dizzy.

The Jem'Hadar on one end of the cargo bay and the Cardassians behind Kira and Rom were firing with rage on their location, unfortunately not at a straight enough range to hurt each other any. There was just enough angle that they could freely fire at the two escaped saboteurs without endangering themselves. The Jem'Hadar were taking the cue of the insulted Cardassians, who were shooting as if there were no end to their weapons charge—and there might not be. Hopelessness stabbed Kira as she realized the enemy soldiers had no reason to preserve power. They were free to take out their frustration until Kira and Rom were roasted like birds on spits.

She gritted her teeth and opened her eyes, then wished she hadn't. A blinding streak of energy cut past her and drilled into the keg Rom was hiding behind. For an instant she saw his astonished face, and a moment later he disappeared in the flash of ignited cargo.

Hot sparks engulfed Kira like a blowing volcano, and she crumpled, waiting to die of raw heat and hopelessness.

Damn the torpedoes—full speed ahead!

Admiral David Glasgow Farragut,
Battle of Mobile Bay, 1864

CHAPTER
16

"THIS WASN'T part of my plan!" Kira gritted her teeth on a piece of melting plastic that flew at her as one of the Jem'Hadar shots nearly cut off her head.

Then there was more fire—more than six weapons. A searing squeal, high-pitched and painful even from a distance.

"Do you hear that?" Rom called through a choking cloud. "That's Bajoran phaser fire!"

He was still alive!

"Why would Dominion troops be using Bajoran weapons?" Kira clung to the sound of her own voice, but she wasn't really expecting an answer from him. Worse fears than her own death now crawled in her stomach—had the Cardassians suspended Odo's Bajoran security squad and confiscated all their weapons? Now to be used against her and Rom and everyone here?

What?

Had the firing stopped?

Her ears were still ringing—she shook her head to clear it. Echoes of the weapons' fire spun upward into the high ceiling of the cargo bay, but then there was no more noise.

She saw Rom peeking at her. Shifting her legs under her, Kira got to one knee, tucked her rifle tight to her ribs, and leaned an inch or two outward.

At the end of the cargo bay stood Odo and two Bajoran guards, their phasers poised over the bodies of the Jem'Hadar guards. At the other entry were two more Bajorans, standing over the crumpled forms of the Cardassians.

"Never underestimate the element of surprise," Odo said proudly. A shy grin tugged at his flat lips.

Shoving hard on a bruised wrist, Kira plunged out from her hiding place, smiling broadly and feeling as if she'd been given a new life.

"Let's go!" She grasped Odo's wrist in a sustaining grip as she rushed between him and his guards. They followed her out, through a passage, and into the habitat ring.

"You have less than forty minutes," Odo called, "to shut down the main computer."

Rom gulped, "I hope that's enough time!"

"It'll have to be," Kira told them, her voice vibrant with determination. Casting a glance at

Odo, she added, "Can you keep the Dominion patrols off our backs?"

"I'll head over to security. I'll create enough false alarms to keep them occupied."

They skidded to a halt at the main computer's conduit access, where Rom instantly yanked off the panel.

"Any questions?" Odo asked, as if he wanted questions.

Kira warmed him with another smile. "I could ask why . . ."

"I don't think I have time to explain it." He seemed to be irritated with himself and disappointed that she hadn't scolded him for his failures in search of the vague and broad. "Besides, I think you know the answer."

She paused, hoping that their forty-minute window could allow for thirty seconds between them. "What about the link?"

He sighed. "The link was paradise . . . but it appears I'm not ready for paradise."

Not much of an explanation. But she didn't really want one. She stepped into the conduit after Rom as Odo picked up the access panel, preparing to close it.

As they paused through a final gaze before the station and the war called again, Odo softly said, "Good luck."

Forgiving him privately, with a look, a smile, Kira said only, "You too."

Deep within the station, less than twenty minutes

later, still warmed by Odo's return to the fold, Kira stood guard over Rom at the conduit juncture of the main computer's core. He had worked in near silence, give or take the occasional curse of self, and Kira finally prodded, "How's it going, Rom?"

"I wish you'd stop asking me that."

"Sorry," she said, even though she hadn't asked before this at all.

"I'm not going to make it . . ."

"Then concentrate on cutting off the power to the station's weapons array. Without weapons, they won't be able to detonate the minefield."

"Not for a while, anyway . . . almost there . . . I just need to decouple the ODN relays . . . just tell me one thing, Major—"

"What's that?"

"When did I grow twelve extra fingers? Because they're all in knots. Why do I think I can do these things? My brother's the smart one. He's the one who knows how to run a business. He's the one who understands why people do the things they do. All I want is the normal number of fingers. Is that too much to ask?"

"I can see the station, Captain," O'Brien called over the crackle and fritz of his damaged panels. "I'll try to get it onto the main screen—there's some of it . . ."

Sisko squinted to look at the main screen, whose milky picture was struggling to focus like a good dog trying to catch a stick that kept bouncing off his snout.

"The minefield!" Bashir came down to Sisko's level and gaped at the screen.

Before them, the previously cloaked minefield now showed at least two-thirds of its mines for the naked eye to see—that meant the cloaking devices had been compromised. With them, the self-replication mechanics would also shut down. Beam upon beam streaked from the distant clamshell of *Deep Space Nine*. Those were the antigraviton beams.

"We're not going to make it," Bashir murmured. "We're not close enough—"

"Quiet, Doctor."

But Sisko knew he was right. They weren't even close to weapon's range.

"Narrate for me, Chief," he requested.

O'Brien's voice was bitter medicine. "Eighty percent of the mines neutralized . . . eighty-three . . . eighty-eight . . . ninety-two percent . . . they'll be able to open fire on the minefield in ten seconds . . ."

"Are we in range?"

"No, sir. Ninety-seven . . . that's it. The mines are neutralized."

The crew fell to silence. Only the bleeping and chittering of ship's systems swirled around their heads. Together they stood inert, with the ship driving itself, and watched as the station that had been their home and base opened fire with a full-power phaser sweep on the dotted Swiss field of green mines blocking the mouth of the wormhole.

In a shimmering show that otherwise would have been grand and beautiful, a series of explosions flickered across space. *Pop, pop, pop, pop*—hundreds of mines blew to bits, one by one, as if each explosion wanted its own applause.

And the minefield fell.

Out of range, out of options.

Jadzia Dax turned and gave Sisko the most embarrassing look he'd ever gotten from a pretty girl. "What do we do now, Captain?"

Somehow the gloom of the moment erupted inside Sisko's mind. Things weren't supposed to happen this way. He had outthought the enemy at a dozen turns. For weeks now he had risen to every challenge. The Federation troops had stood fast against bitter odds and managed to stalemate a virtually unbeatable enemy. Things weren't supposed to be this way—things weren't supposed to come down to a couple of seconds, and then be lost.

This wasn't how legends were made . . . this was how the ugly bits of history were made—the Alamo, Custer's Last Stand, the Six Hundred . . .

I don't want to be one of those stories!

Gritting his teeth, staring with aching eyes at the main screen, he growled, "Take us into the wormhole!"

Plunged in the battery-smoke

. . . .

Right thro' the line they broke.

CHAPTER
17

THE WORMHOLE. An uneasy, unnatural place. Sisko
never liked being inside here. In the not-very-far-
back of his mind was always the possibility that both
ends of this demonic vortex would shut down and
he'd be trapped forever inside.

But those were the nightmares of a man who had
sleep. This—this was something else.

The swirling white maw opened up for them like
an Everest blizzard and swallowed the *Defiant*. On
the screen, they saw the churning mass of energy as
if they were headed down the drain of a sink with the
water running. Once well inside, Sisko braced himself.

"Full stop. Chief, divert all power to forward
shields and weapons."

This was crazy. This was nuts.

"Captain," Dax said, "I'm reading multiple warp signatures ahead."

"On screen, maximum magnification."

So how much magnification was needed to see a thousand Dominion ships flocking toward them in a tubular formation to fit the shape of the wormhole? Not much.

His crew was so quiet . . . saying silent good-byes to each other, he imagined. He would do no such thing. One ship against a thousand was its own good-bye. He only hoped that those Dominion crews would see what this crew was doing and be moved at the pits of their cold-constructed hearts. They would go on and conquer, but perhaps they would always remember.

And those back at *Deep Space Nine* . . . Kira, Odo, Jake . . . even Dukat. They would see. They would remember.

"Lock phasers," he murmured. "Prepare to launch quantum torpedoes."

Before the sound fell, a bright white flash engulfed him. They were hit. Dead.

It felt strange—he was floating. His hands were ten feet from his body. His feet were gone.

Foom . . . foom . . . foom . . . his heartbeat. And his breathing. In. Out. Like a wind tunnel. His lungs were as big as houses.

Other voices, whispering, unintelligible.

Sisko parted his lips, surprised that he still had muscle control. "Why have you brought me here?"

His voice drummed in his skull. He heard the rustling of trees, the crack of a bat on a ball, the roar of a crowd. Home run.

"Show yourselves," he demanded. "What do you want?"

His mind collected itself. He remembered this. He knew what was happening . . . those beings were here, those entities who lived in the wormhole and kept it from closing down . . .

Reality was suddenly elastic. He fought to wrap his mind around what was happening and what wasn't. Why were they interrupting his suicidal sacrifice?

They had talked to him before, these beings. Couldn't rightly call them people. But why now? This was a matter for him and his own kind.

The Sisko has returned to us.

He turned his head. Odo?

No . . . Jake sitting on a barstool. But Odo was here.

He arrives with questions.

Kira . . . and Dukat . . . Damar . . . they were all here. The Promenade. Was that a Vorta over there? They were all talking, one at a time.

There are always questions.

Sisko angrily spoke up. "I didn't ask to come here!"

You desire to end the game.

249

"What game? I don't understand!"

You seek to shed your corporeal existence.

That cannot be allowed.

They were sharing these thoughts. First Kira, then Dukat, then the Vorta, Jake, Odo—they were all speaking, but it wasn't several people he was hearing, or even those of the faces he recognized. Somehow these aliens were using convenient images already in his mind to communicate with him.

The game must not end.

"The game?" Sisko asked. "You mean my life? Is that what this is about? You don't want me to die?"

Maybe an emissary to the Bajoran people was more rare than he thought. Maybe he was worth something to these aliens as much as to the Bajorans they clung to. Why couldn't they just speak up with answers?

The game must continue.

You are the Sisko.

He balled his fists, and was surprised to find the hands were still connected. Something about this, at least, was physical—why did these pompous critters have to be so vague? Did they think that meant they were profound? Hardly! Vague was vague! Why didn't they say something that made sense! Were they waiting for a mere mortal to tease it out of them?

"Believe me, I don't want to die," he said flatly. "But I have to do everything I can to prevent the Dominion from conquering the Alpha Quadrant. If that means sacrificing my life and the lives of my crew, so be it!"

And if it didn't fit into their idea of an overreaching scheme, then too bad.

We do not agree.

We find your reasoning flawed.

Insufficient.

Why couldn't he just punch one of them in the nose?

"I'm flattered that you feel that way," he snapped, "but it doesn't change anything. Now send me back to my ship."

The scene changed. Bridge of the *Defiant*. Flat as a theater set.

As if scolding a child, Sisko grumbled, "This isn't what I meant. I want to return to my reality."

You are the Sisko.

As if he didn't know his own name. He was the annoyed Sisko. The impatient Sisko. The quit-interfering-with-my-reality Sisko.

"I'm also a Starfleet captain," he insisted. "I have a job to do and I intend to do it."

The Sisko is belligerent.

Aggressive.

Adversarial.

"You're damned right I'm adversarial! You have no right to interfere in my life!"

We have every right.

"Fine! You want to interfere, then interfere! Do something about those Dominion reinforcements!"

That is a corporeal matter.

Corporeal matters do not concern us.

What bilge. Now he had them. What liars.

"The hell they don't," Sisko charged. "What about Bajor? You can't tell me Bajor doesn't concern you. You've sent the Bajorans orbs and emissaries, you've encouraged them to create an entire religion around you—you even told me once that *you* were 'of Bajor'! So don't tell me you're not concerned with 'corporeal matters'!"

He moved around the table—when had that appeared?—and walked through the aliens who were pretending to look like people he knew. They weren't looking at him.

"I don't want to see Bajor destroyed," he went on with boiling force, "and neither do you. And we all know that's exactly what's going to happen if the Dominion takes over the Alpha Quadrant. You say you don't want me to sacrifice my life? Fine! Neither do I! You want to be gods? Then be gods! I need a miracle! Bajor needs a miracle! Stop those ships!"

The scene around him blurred. He heard voices, disjointed words, flashing thoughts. Were they speaking to each other on some distant plane?

control . . . penance . . . path . . . follow the path . . .

"What path is that?" he called into the flickering void. "What path is that? What are you saying? Where is my miracle?"

"Torpedoes locked. Targets locked."

Sisko looked around. The crew, as he had left them—but had he left at all? Was he dead or dreaming? Were these the last seconds as his body fell apart in disruption?

"Here they come!"

Dax's voice was dreadfully near.

Seizing himself by the mind, Sisko shook off the visions still rolling in his head and snapped, "Fire on my command. Steady, people. Make every shot count . . ."

Closer, closer—the Dominion fleet pressed toward the one tiny ship.

"Benjamin!" Dax again, surprised.

Energy bolts rocketed past them from the sides of the wormhole's internal structure. Wild, uncontrolled viral energy crackled from ship to ship. From outside to in, the Dominion ships began to fade away as if they were paintings being washed out by a big brush.

"They've cloaked," O'Brien gasped.

Dax looked at her panel. "I'm not picking up any neutrino emissions—"

Garak stared at the screen. "Then where did they go?"

His legs shuddering, Sisko began slowly to understand what he was seeing.

"Wherever they went," he said, "I don't think they're coming back . . ."

"What happened?" O'Brien came out from behind his panel and gaped at the empty screen. "What in hell happened to them?"

As they all stared at the empty swirl of energy where a moment ago a deadly fleet had swarmed, Ben Sisko felt a bizarre peace flow over him from his toes to the top of his skull.

"Hell's own miracle, Chief," he said quietly. "I guess gods don't like to be scolded."

Storm'd at with shot and shell, . .
While horse and hero fell,
They that had fought so well
Came thro' the jaws of Death,
Back from the mouth of Hell,
All that was left of them,
Left of six hundred.

CHAPTER
18

"THE *DEFIANT!*"

Damar's cry narrated the sudden opening of the wormhole on the main screens and in the large viewports as Dukat turned to look. Beside him, Weyoun and the female shapeshifter also watched, incredulous and hopeful.

Dukat pressed closer to the vision. "Our reinforcements must be right behind . . ."

Whir, whir, whir—and the wormhole closed up again with a brilliant flash.

"No, sir," Damar said, scanning his readouts. "There's no sign of them!"

No readings, no emissions, no signatures—

"That's impossible!" Weyoun gasped. "Check our listening posts in the Gamma Quadrant!"

"They're not there either."

"But they entered the wormhole," Dukat protested. "Where could they be?"

Damar turned confused eyes to him. "I don't know—the *Defiant* has opened fire on us!"

"Destroy it!"

On Dukat's order, Damar hammered at the weapons panel. Not a thing happened. Nothing.

"What's the matter, Damar?"

"Our weapons are off-line!"

"How can that be?"

Gritting his teeth, Damar anticipated, "Major Kira."

"But she's in custody!"

"It *must* be her or some part of that sabotage unit!"

"Call security!"

Damar pounded again, blinked at the monitors, then gulped, "You see? They've escaped from the cell! Rom and Kira—they must've had help!"

Ready to pull Damar's jaw apart, Dukat held himself in check somehow and Damar apparently saw the great danger of suggesting that Ziyal must be involved. What mattered was that the rebels had escaped and their weapons were down. This was no coincidence. And Kira could be very thorough.

"Can you get our weapons back on line?" he demanded.

"Not for a while. Sir—two hundred enemy ships

have broken through our lines. They're headed this way!"

Too much, too much. Dukat felt his body collapse with realization of what the past few seconds meant.

Weyoun broke into an inexplicable smile. "Well, time to start packing."

The female shapeshifter showed no reaction except perhaps to straighten her shoulders a little as she turned to Damar. "Contact our forces in the Alpha Quadrant and tell them to fall back to Cardassian territory. It appears this war is going to take longer than expected."

"I'll meet you at airlock five," Weyoun told her, and just like that the two of them faded mistily away.

Just like that!

Stunned, Damar turned to Dukat. "Sir?"

Dukat stared into open space through the main viewport, shaking his head, staring, shaking, staring—he pressed a hand to his forehead and with the other hand he fondled the baseball. Sisko's baseball. The baseball was laughing at him. It had grown a little face and was sneering at him.

"Victory was within our grasp . . ."

"We have to evacuate the station, sir!"

"Bajor . . . the Federation . . . the Alpha Quadrant . . . all lost . . ."

"We have to go now, sir!"

"Go?"

"The Federation ships," Damar gasped. "They'll be here soon! We have to get to Cardassia!"

Dukat almost nodded. Suddenly he shook himself and bolted for the turbolift. "I have to find my daughter!"

Damar grasped his arm roughly. "I'll send someone for her!"

Dignity. Honor. Poise. "That won't be necessary."

Dukat stepped into the turbolift, concentrating his thoughts down to one small goal. Ziyal. He had to find Ziyal.

"You're wasting your time," Damar told him as the door began to close. As the turbolift sank into the body of the station, Dukat heard Damar's fading last call right through the metal walls—

"She won't go with you . . ."

The words echoed in his head. Lost. All was lost. He had to get Ziyal, and then he wouldn't be lost. The others were all leaving. The Jem'Hadar ships would soon peel away from the station and run. Weyoun would run. The female Founder would go hide in the Cardassian system, masquerading as a jug of soap or something. They were all running.

Yes, everyone had to run sooner or later. This would not be the first time he had left Terok Nor . . . it would not be the last.

Yet his heart was cold, as if it had stopped beating and stood waiting for orders. Run, run, everybody run.

The habitat ring opened before him and the turbolift spat him out like chewed waste. Where was she? In their quarters? He would find her. He would cling to her. She was the last possession he had. She was his reason to go on. She was his only future—his daughter—the one thing in the universe he might have done right.

"Father!"

"Ziyal!"

They ran toward each other. She didn't hate him! He could see in her face that she had forgiven him!

"I've been looking for you," she said quickly. "I heard about the evacuation."

Feeling his face brighten, Dukat gazed at her and grasped her arms. She still cared for him! Victory!

"You're all I have," he told her. "All I care about."

She smiled. "No matter how much I try to hate you, I can't."

"I couldn't live with myself if you hated me," he said sincerely. He grasped her elbow. "Come—we'll talk on the way home."

Her expression changed. "Home?"

"Cardassia," he said. "We have to leave here, before the Federation arrives."

But she pulled against his grip. "I'm not leaving," she declared.

Dukat stared at her, chilled by a sudden fear. "These people are our enemies!"

"They're not *my* enemies," she said. "I'm one of them."

"That's not true."

"Father," Ziyal insisted, her eyes very clear, "I

helped Major Kira and the others escape from the holding cells."

No, no, this was one of Damar's silly accusations. This was a joke, and Ziyal was cheerful enough to help pull it on her father, her precious father who had learned to love her. Yes, that was it. She was joking, teasing.

Dukat swallowed, then again. "Do you know what you're saying?"

"Yes, I do," she told him firmly. "I belong here. Good-bye, Father . . . I love you . . ."

She stepped away from him, putting a gap between them as if to declare her position. No, no, this was not right. Dukat reached for her. He smiled, he took a step—

She gazed at him with the oddest expression. A crease of pain, wonder in her eyes, confusion . . . a flash . . . a gaping hole opened up in her chest . . . her arms flared slightly as she was propelled backward away from Dukat.

His fingers scratched the air to catch her, but she shot away from him.

"No!" he screamed.

He spun around.

At first he saw nothing, no one, but then Damar stepped out from behind an archway. His sidearm was raised. A phaser.

"You heard her," Damar said. "She's a traitor."

Shivering, Dukat dropped at his daughter's side

and collected her into his arms. The gash in her chest steamed and sizzled as the remnant energy from the phaser hit continued to burn through her body. Under his hand, he felt her spine fuse and her muscles convulse.

"I forgive you," he murmured. "Do you hear me, Ziyal? It's all right . . . it's all right . . ."

A pair of legs appeared at his side. Damar was looking down at them. "We're out of time, sir. The last ship is waiting for us."

Feeling Damar clasp his arm and try to pull him away, Dukat yanked fiercely until the grip was broken. "I love you, Ziyal . . . do you hear me? I love you!"

Soon the legs were gone and all he heard was Damar's retreating footsteps and the ragged, sucking breaths of air rushing directly from his lips into Ziyal's open wound and into her lungs. He could breathe for her . . . he could keep her alive. His love could keep her alive. His promises. Their future. She would live. She would be alive. She would paint him a flower.

"I love you," he murmured, rocking her in his arms. "I love you, Ziyal . . . I'm going to conquer the quadrant for you . . . all of Bajor will bow at your feet . . . you'll be a princess . . . you'll be a queen . . . no—no—much more than Bajor will worship you. A hundred planets will know your name . . . you'll never be lonely or frightened again . . . Ziyal? You're so cold . . . let me get my arms around you. I'll tell you about the future . . . our future together . . . you won't leave me . . . you know I can change for you. I can change, Ziyal . . . I can change . . . I can win, Ziyal . . . your father can win . . . we'll go back to Cardassia . . . we'll be safe there. You'll live with me, father and daughter . . . everything will be fine . . . everything will be wonderful . . ."

Captain's Log, Stardate unspecified, destruct situation entry. Charles W. Reynolds recording on behalf of the crew of the U.S.S. Centaur.

I'm not good at this sort of thing, Admiral, so I'll make it short. If you're hearing this tape, then myself and my crew are dead in the line of duty. In just a few hours we're going to storm the Dominion lines with the rest of the armada, so if I haven't amended this, it's a good bet that's where we bought the farm. Guess I don't believe it's my time to go, or I wouldn't be so flip about it, would I?

On to business. I've shipped the personal logs, wills, and personal effects of my crewmen back to Starbase 375 on a passing private supply ship called the *Bernadine Cook*. It's a real dependable ship with a captain I've known for about a decade. Ought to arrive in about four days with all our stuff. I also left a few mementos we usually keep on board here, but no sense taking things we care about into a withering battle. Just leave everything on the *Cook* and I'll be sure to pick them up when we get back to home space.

In that pack is a personal tape to my wife and my kids . . . gave me the squirms to record a thing like that. If we're just lost without a trace out here, be sure not to send that tape home to Blue Rocket before you're absolutely sure we're not landed on a scrubby planet in survival mode or floating around in one of the pods. I don't want my family to hear that tape only to have me show up later like some kind of a zombie. If it's at all possible, I mean if he doesn't have too much of a mess to clean up at the wormhole, I wonder if Ben Sisko wouldn't mind explaining everything to my wife? I mean, he knows what it's like to have a wife and a family, and there aren't that many Starfleet lifers who bother with that kind of anchorage—I guess I should probably edit this later, shouldn't I? Just talking off the top of my head.

You know, I never used to think the hard few years we've had on the ol' *Centaur,* trying to settle Blue Rocket and build up colonial stability and some security, but it's always just been struggle and strife, not really life-or-death danger. There really hasn't been this kind of threat in years and years. War's something different, isn't it? Funny how it gets easier to face death when you got the idea you're doing some real good. All of us here, we all feel like that, I want you to know. We all do.

I'm lousy at this, aren't I? Well, I'll sign off and hope nobody ever has to listen to this. I just want to tell you, sir, and especially Ben Sisko one thing . . . thanks for letting us in on the hot action. Us colony builders, we don't very often get to feel as if we're heroes.

Thanks, Admiral, and thanks to you too, Ben. Thanks for that feeling.

I'll see you both at *Deep Space Nine*. Charlie Reynolds, out.

The glorious sounds of cheering—what a wonderful noise!

Even before the airlock opened, Sisko heard the cheers. Before the doors opened he heard Jake's voice shouting some vocal joy or other. He heard Quark—and that was Rom's voice. Alive—they were alive.

And laughter. He heard that too.

Finally, finally the pressure equalized and the doors opened and he piled out into the arms of his friends. Behind him were Dax, O'Brien, Nog, Garak, Bashir, and the rest of *Defiant*'s crew, none quite as dead as they had shortly ago expected. Every clap on the shoulder, every handshake, every hug, was secondary until he got his arms around his son. Damn, this kid was tall!

And Odo appeared over Jake's shoulder as Sisko smiled so hard his face hurt.

"Welcome back, Captain," the shapeshifter said.

"It's good to see you, Odo," Sisko told him, then scanned all the others. "It's good to see all of you!"

The other airlock chunked open and out came General Martok and Commander Worf, flanked by a gush of Klingons. This was their victory party too.

"Worf!" Dax broke away from the crowd and ran into her fiancé's arms. "I guess the wedding's still on!"

Martok lumbered to Sisko and roared, "It appears I owe you a barrel of blood wine!"

"We'll drink it together, General."

He paused, surveyed the reunions going on all around him. O'Brien, Quark, Bashir . . . Rom and his wife greeting Nog and seeing the new uniforms . . . someone was missing.

In all the flurry, it actually took a few seconds for him to isolate what he was thinking.

"Where's Major Kira?" he asked.

Beside him, Jake's smile dropped away. "She's in the infirmary. With Ziyal."

"Ziyal? Was she injured?"

As the crowd dissipated and various joyous people went in their own directions to jump-start their lives on the station, Sisko looked into Jake's youthful face, and saw Odo's plastic expression beyond. Over his shoulder, Martok waited for the answer too, understanding the complexities of this particular turn.

"Maybe Bashir can help," Sisko suggested.

Odo lowered his gaze. "Perhaps . . . but he would be of more assistance for Dukat, Captain."

"Dukat? He's still here?"

"Yes, sir."

"Where? Take me to him."

"This way."

Joy was put on suspension, but Sisko clung to his son on one side and the presence of Odo on the other as they hurried through the station, letting Odo lead them. On the way, both Jake and Odo told him of the adventures they'd had here. Tension. Resistance. Secret meetings. Plots. Espionage. Sabotage. Sentences of execution. Escape. More sabotage. Damar and a phaser, loaded with desperation.

Sisko heard all this with great interest, and wondered what was being left out. The bittersweet juice of victory at great cost flooded his veins instead of blood. He had no blood—it had all been shed out there, drained from the bodies of all those who had given their lives so he could walk here today. He had many captain's logs to listen to, many requests to fulfill. He wondered how much it would hurt and if he still had that much courage left. Whose voices would he hear?

Odo led the way not to the infirmary, but straight past it to the holding cells of the security corridor. Why?

They went inside the main vestibule. Before them lay the cells. In one cell, protected by a low-grade forcefield, Gul Dukat sat crumpled on the deck, muttering to himself.

"We'll go back to Cardassia . . . we'll live together . . . father and daughter . . . I know you forgive me . . . After all, I am your father . . . and I forgive you."

Gripped with unexpected sympathy, Sisko gazed upon his strong and worthy opponent. Death, perhaps. But no soldier wished this on another.

Sisko nodded to Odo. Without a word he gave permission for this poor man to be taken to Bashir and treated . . . if this could be treated.

Odo silently keyed off the forcefield. Inside the cell, Dukat did not respond with so much as a flinch. He just kept on murmuring.

"I forgive you, I forgive you."

Uttering pointless reassurances, and using a touch so gentle that Sisko was surprised to see it, Odo lifted the once-powerful nemesis to his feet. Dukat gazed at Odo briefly, beseechingly, as if he didn't understand the face he saw.

As Odo led him past Sisko, Dukat paused. The once lucid eyes were tepid and glazed.

"I forgive you too," the Cardassian leader uttered. He reached for Sisko's hand, and into it he pressed the baseball Sisko had left behind in the office.

Like a child giving up a teddy bear, Dukat raised his chin and fought for a shred of common dignity as he shuffled away in Odo's grip.

Sisko watched them go. He tossed the ball into the air and caught it. So that was that.

"You did it, Dad . . . you won."

Oh—Jake was still here.

Reluctant to take this particular laud, perhaps reluctant to take the very last of Dukat's hopes and burning it to a cinder, Sisko simply said, "I had some help. Besides, this war isn't over yet." He turned to his son and threw an arm around his knobby shoulders. "But let's worry about that tomorrow. Right now, it's just good to be home."

And he tossed the ball. And he caught it.

Look for STAR TREK Fiction from Pocket Books

Star Trek®: The Original Series

Star Trek: The Next Generation®

Star Trek: Deep Space Nine®

Star Trek®: Voyager™

Flashback • Diane Carey
Mosaic • Jeri Taylor

Star Trek®: New Frontier

Star Trek®: Day of Honor

Star Trek®: The Captain's Table

Book One: *War Dragons* • L. A. Graf
Book Two: *Dujonian's Hoard* • Michael Jan Friedman
Book Three: *The Mist* • Dean W. Smith & Kristine K. Rusch
Book Four: *Fire Ship* • Diane Carey
Book Five: *Once Burned* • Peter David
Book Six: *Where Sea Meets Sky* • Jerry Oltion

Star Trek®: The Dominion War

Book One: *Behind Enemy Lines* • John Vornholt
Book Two: *Call to Arms . . .* • Diane Carey
Book Three: *Tunnel Through the Stars* • John Vornholt
Book Four: *. . . Sacrifice of Angels* • Diane Carey

1252.01